She's Just a Little Amish Girl
A Gettysburg Novel

David Bachman

Black Rose Writing | Texas

First printing

ISBN: 978-1-68513-611-6
LIBRARY OF CONGRESS CONTROL NUMBER: 2024952271
PUBLISHED BY BLACK ROSE WRITING
www.blackrosewriting.com

Printed in the United States of America
Suggested Retail Price (SRP) $17.95

She's Just a Little Amish Girl is printed in Minion Pro

*As a planet-friendly publisher, Black Rose Writing does its best to eliminate unnecessary waste to reduce paper usage and energy costs, while never compromising the reading experience. As a result, the final word count vs. page count may not meet common expectations.

She's Just a
Little Amish Girl

Chapter One
1860
A Visit to Cashtown

Rebekah smiled as she sat next to her father on their farm wagon. An early fall sun was shining on the fertile fields and on the forested slopes of South Mountain a few miles in the distance. But the idyllic scenery of the Pennsylvanian farm country was hiding mounting tensions among their neighbors. Rebekah did not know about the brewing conflict that would soon have a brother taking up arms against brother and neighbor fighting neighbor. To her, everything seemed right with the world this Saturday morning in 1860.

As a ten-year-old girl whose two younger brothers were quickly growing into young men, she didn't get to accompany her father on his weekly trips into Cashtown as often as she used to. These days, Caleb Stutzman was more likely to bring Zephaniah or Ezekiel with him, which was natural for an Amish father to do. Every week he took chickens, eggs, milk, vegetables, fruit and sometimes preserved food in jars to the Cashtown Inn. Jacob Mickley, the owner of the inn, aimed to see his place regarded as the best on Chambersburg Pike, which ran between Gettysburg and Chambersburg, so he wanted to serve the best local food he could find.

That morning at breakfast, Rebekah's mother had asked Caleb which of the energetic and mischievous boys, seven and six years old, he planned to take with him. Rebekah thought back to the day before and tried to remember if either had been ordered to haul in firewood for the stove, which was her father's usual punishment for misbehavior. If that was the case, the other brother would be chosen to accompany him to Cashtown. But her father, "Daed", as his Amish children called him, after a long pause, replied, "I will take Rebekah. There may be some trouble in town, and I will need her to help steady the horses."

Rebekah noticed nothing special as they approached the little town, which comprised several dozen houses, a few stores, several churches and, at the far end, at the base of South Mountain, the Cashtown Inn. Rebekah looked forward to seeing Mr. Mickley's cook, a black man who seldom ventured far from the steps that led down to the kitchen of the Inn, which was in the basement. He always helped unload the wagon with her father and then carried the goods down into the kitchen. He always smiled at her and asked about her kittens. Rebekah turned to her father as they passed the first houses and said, "I sure am happy that you brought me today, Daed."

Below his furrowed brow, her father kept his eyes fixed on the road ahead. Then suddenly, as though he had just heard her, he turned and smiled at her, gently patting her bonnet. "Rebekah, I've heard that the English in town are all stirred up. When we stop at Mr. Mickley's, please step down from the wagon and hold the reins of the horses and keep them steady."

Rebekah didn't understand why this Saturday would differ from any other in the peaceful farming village. But as they drove farther into town, her heart beat faster. Something was indeed different this Saturday morning, very different. It seemed like everyone who lived in the town was out on the road. They stood talking to each other in pairs or larger groups. The "English," as the Amish—who spoke their own dialect of Pennsylvania German among themselves—called non-Amish people, typically chatted about their farms, businesses, children and other aspects of ordinary country life. But today, there was only angry shouting.

Rebekah instinctively slid a little closer to her father, who carefully steered the wagon around a group of men arguing in the middle of the road. She had never seen men so angry, and many of the women they passed seemed upset as well. As they neared the Cashtown Inn, she realized the Pike was filled with people, and in the middle of the crowd, she noticed a young woman in a different style of dress holding a stack of papers that she was passing out to the townsfolk. Some people took them and read them. Others crinkled them up and threw them on the ground, or back at the woman who had handed them out.

As her father steered the wagon around the edge of the crowd, Rebekah could make out some of the conversation being bantered back and forth.

"Damn abolitionists, gonna get a war started!" a burly farmer yelled.

Another shouted to no one in particular, "I ain't got no slaves, but I ain't gonna die for no darkies neither!"

A younger man between them yelled back, "Slavery is an ungodly sin, and it's a reproach on the entire nation!"

Yet another man exclaimed, "When Abe Lincoln gets elected next month, he'll end this slavery curse," to which another yelled back, "Yeah, by gettin' us into a damn war!"

Rebekah turned back, curious to comprehend what was being said. She had heard of Abraham Lincoln, and knew he was trying to win the election, but knew very little else about him. She did not know what an abolitionist was. Her roaming thoughts were shocked back into the present by her father's gentle tug on her arm. Pulling the frightened girl around to him, he peered meaningfully at her and said, "Rebekah, child, that is their world. It is not ours." It was a message often spoken around her home and with their friends and family. The contrast between the peaceful way the Amish talked to each other and the bitter words she was hearing in Cashtown that morning could not be more striking, and she did not want to be part of their type of living.

"Rebekah, when we get to the inn, I will pull along the side porch by the stairs to the basement. Please get out and hold the horses and keep them calm while I try to find Mr. Mickley and Elijah." He steered the wagon around, so its rear gate was close to the basement stairs. As her father left in search of Mr. Mickley, Rebekah climbed down from the wagon and went to the front of the horses, gently gathering the reins as she stood in front of them. She caressed their muzzles to reassure them. Having been around horses her whole young life, she realized that the boisterous crowd had alarmed them as much as it had her. Looking over the wagon, she noticed Elijah walking slowly up the stairs, but he stopped a few steps from the top. He seemed different today, a little preoccupied and nervous, as he watched the boisterous crowd down the street. He glanced at Rebekah and nodded a polite "hello" but did not speak or come over to her. She waved silently back at him.

After a few minutes, Rebekah noticed the crowd was getting louder and moving toward the Inn. Not wanting to disappoint her father, she kept her eyes focused on the horses. But as she heard the uproar moving toward her, she turned toward the crowd. The woman with the papers walked briskly toward the steps on the side porch of the inn when a young man standing on the bottom step pushed her backwards. She turned away and shouted, "Maybe you don't care about slavery, but I'm a human being, and I do care!"

A moment later, she was standing directly in front of Rebekah and handed her one of the papers that she was carrying. "Please read this," she insisted and turned away.

"But I'm not allowed to read newspapers," Rebekah replied.

The woman looked up, irritated, but then noticed from Rebekah's bonnet that she was Amish. Knowing that the Amish went to school but did not study ideas and events outside their community, she hastily said, "Okay, I'm Sarah. I'm an abolitionist from Philadelphia and I'm—"

"What's an abolitionist?" Rebekah interrupted.

"We want to abolish, or get rid of, slavery in the South. See this picture?" she said as she pointed to the drawing on the pamphlet Rebekah had in her hand. "These people are Negroes. They're from Africa and they are slaves in the Southern states. This man is being whipped, this woman is crying, and this little boy is being sold to somebody else, never to see his family again. This must stop; we need to stop it!"

Rebekah suddenly felt short of breath. The evil the picture depicted seemed to reach out from the paper and grab her. She thought of her family and how, despite any temporary disagreements they might have, they all loved each other deeply. It was incomprehensible to her that someone would tear them apart. She thought of Moses in the Bible, whose people were the Pharaoh's slaves in Egypt, but she couldn't believe something like that could happen in America.

Rebekah wanted to know more. She had to know more. "Wh-what are their names?"

The woman had moved away from the wagon, but the compassion in Rebekah's voice drew her back. Many of the people in Cashtown that morning had told her they agreed with her and encouraged her to keep it up, but did not offer to get involved. Others became infuriated and refused to read the pamphlets. A few of the rougher men had accused her of being a "darkie" herself. But none of the people in Cashtown had asked her the names of the family pictured on the leaflet.

"You mean the people in the drawing? Their names don't matter. It's happening all over the South!" she blurted out, but noting Rebekah's imploring eyes, she quickly changed her tone and replied in a somewhat softer tone, "The father is Amos, the mother is Hannah, and the little boy is Moses." The woman turned away and instantly forgot the names she had made up to satisfy the little Amish girl. She couldn't know that as Rebekah studied the picture, she would never, ever forget the names of Amos, Hannah, and little Moses. Her imagination added to the picture ideas about their lives, their feelings, their past and their future. All she knew of them, all she knew of Africa, all she knew of Negroes in the South, of slavery, was what the abolitionist had just told her. What she didn't know didn't matter to her. All that mattered to her was that Amos was being whipped, Hannah was crying, and Moses was being sold, and something had to be done about it.

Her life, she thought, would never be the same.

Rebekah's father quickly shattered her thoughts as he ripped the paper from her hands, glaring at Rebekah. It made her heart stop, and tears welled in her eyes.

"I told you not to talk to anybody!" he scolded her angrily.

"But she handed it to me!" Rebekah cried, trembling, realizing that she had never seen her father so agitated.

"You are a little Amish girl! This stuff does not matter to you! I've told you before, we don't get mixed up with the English and their ungodly arguments," he harshly told her in their dialect. They climbed back on their wagon, and he snapped the reins, shaking his head.

Rebekah fought hard to hold back her tears, and yet she could not take her mind off the picture, aghast at the horror of it. Her despair matched her conviction that something needed to be done to stop it. But what could she do? As the wagon turned out onto the Pike, Rebekah looked back toward the basement stairs of the Inn. Elijah was standing still, a box of eggs in his hands. When their eyes met, he slowly nodded his head up and down, confirming to Rebekah that what the abolitionist had said was true. Rebekah wondered if he had been a slave at one time. She had never thought to ask him. Her father had always talked to him politely and treated him no differently than he treated any of the other English, so she had as well. But was this why he stayed close to the basement kitchen? And was this why he was so alarmed that morning? Was he scared that some of the angry men would make him a slave?

All these thoughts were on Rebekah's mind as her father drove away from the Inn. His uncharacteristically angry tone had abated, and he steered the wagon back towards their farm. Rebekah assumed he was heading straight home, but he stopped in front of the general store. Caleb Stutzman was also very upset about what had just happened at the Inn, especially the way he had raised his voice to Rebekah. Emma, his wife, had noticed that despite his love for all five of his children, he had a special place in his heart for Rebekah. He never said it to anyone, but the thought had occurred to him in the past that he wished she had been born a boy, because he recognized a powerful spirit in her. Turning toward Rebekah, he said in a low, almost apologetic tone,

"Rebekah, Liebchen, I need to buy some sugar for your mother. Please stay on the wagon." He added, slowly: "And … talk … to … no one."

Looking through the door of the general store, she saw Mr. Yoder and his two boys coming out. She counted the sacks of sugar the boys were carrying. Another good crop for Mr. Yoder, she thought. Then she heard Mr. Yoder call out as he stepped through the door, "So, it's the Stutzman wagon! I suppose your daed's leg is all healed up now, ja?"

Rebekah acknowledged him with a polite nod and a quick smile, but then looked away. She would not get into more trouble with her father for talking to him, of all people. She remembered last fall that Mr. Yoder told her father how she'd slapped his boys while all the children in the Amish community were picking apples at Grandma Werner's orchard. That had cost her three licks from her father's belt before she could explain that they had pulled her hair first.

As Mr. Yoder went back into the store to settle his account, one of his sons said to Rebekah, "My mamm's going to make a bunch of fine apple cakes with this sugar, but we won't give you any!"

She totally ignored their jeers, thinking silently that they were such brats. With a little smirk, she remembered she didn't even know their names, and she intended for it to stay that way. Her two older sisters, fourteen-year-old Ruth and thirteen-year-old Mary, seemed to always be whispering about boys when they were alone in their bedroom. Rebekah, who shared their room, was never invited into the conversation, and she was happy to be excluded. They were at the age when they were looking forward to being courted by young men in the Amish community around Cashtown. Rebekah shook her head at the thought that someday Mr. and Mrs. Yoder might encourage one of their sons to consider courting "that younger Stutzman girl".

Rebekah smiled at her father as he emerged from the store. She was proud of him. Caleb Stutzman grew up near Lancaster, a town further east, and moved to this area, eager to find available land and eager to settle down with a good wife. He had worked hard and earned as much money as he could, and more importantly, earned the respect of a young Amish woman named Emma and her parents. With the money he had saved and some money from Emma's parents, he had purchased an abandoned farm on the gentle hills just east of Cashtown. The house sat on the south side of the road, with the wooden barn on the opposite side. The ground behind the barn sloped gently down toward Marsh Creek, a tree-lined brook. A dirt ramp sloped up from the road to the large sliding doors on the upper level of the barn. To the right side of the barn was a well-kept chicken coop. The rear wall of the barn basement had a small single door for people to walk through and a large sliding door that was used to bring animals into the lower floor. The main floor of the barn extended over the rear basement wall of the barn, creating a dry space below for storage and work. Caleb called this space, known to farmers as a forebay, his workshop. Like all farmers, he had a wide variety of skills. Emma often said of him, "He can fix anything."

"It is a good place to raise corn and kids," she had heard her father say over and over about their farm. The Stutzman farm was typical for the area: about seventy acres, on which they grew corn, hay, and oats, and raised chickens, pigs and a few dairy cows.

Caleb was a quiet man, hardworking and dedicated to his Amish faith. He would have preferred to settle farther east in Lancaster, where he grew up, where virtually everybody was Amish. But the land prices were too high there. When Rebekah was five years old, her grandfather came to live with them, and it was he who taught her how to handle farm animals, particularly the horses. Her mother was somewhat bothered by her daughter taking on that role, but with her two young sons too small to help in the barn, and with all the work that needed to be done, she did not protest to Caleb. Even after her grandfather passed away in the winter of 1858, Rebekah spent a lot of her time in the barn. She learned to milk the cows, herd the chickens into their roosts, and most importantly, to take care of the horses. She could see in her father's eyes how thankful he was for her willingness to work hard and take responsibility.

As she grew older, she recognized that most Amish girls weren't so interested in working in the barn and with the animals. But she felt more at home in the barn compared to the house. Just before the spring of 1860, Caleb had decided to build a side porch on the house, right off the kitchen door. But before he could finish, he slipped off the roof on a snowy day and broke his leg. Not being able to plow the fields that spring was a source of great anxiety for the family, and even with her skills with their horses, that task was too much for Rebekah. But people learned about her father's injury, and after the other Amish farmers finished their fields, they helped to plant the Stutzman fields. They asked for no payment. That was not the Amish way—and the gratitude in Caleb's eyes and a hearty lunch brought out to them in the fields by Rebekah was all the compensation they wanted. Rebekah had to admit that while she sometimes quietly questioned some aspects of the Amish faith, the manner in which the members of their community helped her family out in their time of trouble was evidence of their godliness.

Chapter Two
1860-1863, A Faraway War

Over the next three years, Rebekah's daily life changed, especially when she finished her schooling in reading and arithmetic at the one-room Amish school down the road. She excelled in school and her mother also taught her the skills every good Amish girl should know. She learned to sew, to stitch quilts, grow and preserve vegetables, cook healthy meals, and keep a clean and tidy home. Her mother even sat her down one Saturday when she and her father had come back from Cashtown to show her how she kept track of the money that Caleb brought back. Rebekah marveled at how smart she was at so many things. She also loved the slow singing at the worship meetings held at alternating Amish homes on Sundays, where afterward she might spend a little time playing with the other Amish children as the adults visited. She even began to understand why Ruth and Mary had always whispered about boys, especially since Ruth was now planning her wedding. Boys, Rebekah thought, turn out to be something more than just nuisances. Boys, that is, except for the Yoder brothers, who consistently irritated her whenever she saw them.

But Rebekah Stutzman was, in one way, different from other Amish children. Her curiosity led her to be at least somewhat aware of events happening in her country beyond her safe, quiet community. She knew Abraham Lincoln was President and that he didn't like slavery. She knew that the Southern States became very upset with him and pulled out of the United States and started their own country, the Confederate States of America. On trips to Cashtown, she overheard people talk and argue about ideas like federal authority and state's rights. She did not really understand what those words meant. The only thing that mattered to her was that if the Confederate States had their way, slavery would continue. And to Rebekah Stutzman of Cashtown, Pennsylvania, that meant that Amos was getting whipped, Hannah was crying, and Moses was being sold. She cried for that to stop; she prayed it would stop, and she hoped it would stop.

Sometimes Rebekah tried very hard to forget about slavery and the war that was being fought over it. It occurred to her that the lives of Ruth, Mary, and the other Amish children were much simpler than hers, because they did not dwell on such heart wrenching thoughts. She especially enjoyed Sundays, the day of worship, the day that all the Amish people in her community got together at one of their farms. Rebekah wished she could be like the other children, unburdened by the thoughts of the destructive war being fought in the land. She enjoyed bathing in the love of her community and yearned for more peaceful times. But then the images of Amos, Hannah, and Moses returned to her mind, and the unrest in her heart as well.

Rebekah understood that war had broken out, and that many battles had been fought at places like Manassas, Antietam, Fredericksburg, and Shiloh, but she had no idea where those places were. She had heard men in Cashtown talk about all the people, steel, money, and railroads that the North had. They insisted that with all those advantages, the North would eventually defeat Robert E. Lee and the Confederacy. She didn't understand any of that, but she understood that the war was about slavery, and whether it would continue.

One day in 1862, on another trip to the Cashtown Inn, she got up her courage and asked Elijah if he had been a slave. As if someone had punched him in the stomach, he exhaled loudly and lowered his head. When he lifted his head back up and looked at Rebekah, he paused and then nodded slowly. Rebekah then asked him, "How did you get to Mr. Mickley's, then? Surely, you're not his slave!"

"Oh, no! I'm not a slave here. Mr. Mickley treats me fine." Then, nodding toward the Chambersburg Pike climbing up South Mountain to the west, he continued, "I escaped my master in Virginia and snuck my way through Maryland, and with the help of some real fine Quaker folk in Chambersburg, I got across the border into Pennsylvania. Slavery ain't allowed here, so I am a free man, as long as none of them slave-catchers comes lookin' for me. A friend of the Quakers, a man who travels a lot, told the Quakers that Mr. Mickley needed a cook, and so he brought me here." A smile came to Elijah's face, and he added, "When that man comes through and stays here, I give him an enormous plate of food!"

Rebekah just stood and looked at him for a few moments, peering intently into his eyes. Then she asked quietly, "Elijah, did your master ever whip you?"

He dropped his head, and when he looked up, she saw tears in his big brown eyes as he nodded. "Rebekah, no man wants to work the fields for another man in that heat without getting paid or even getting enough to eat. They must whip colored folks to get them to work like that."

Mr. Mickley and her father interrupted them when they emerged from behind the house. Her father then handed his farm produce down to Elijah from the back of the wagon.

Tears rolled down Rebekah's cheeks as she turned and climbed back up on the wagon seat. *It's true*, she thought. *Just like the abolitionist's pamphlet.* In her despair, she hardly noticed that Caleb had climbed back onto the wagon seat beside her. "What is wrong, Liebchen?" he asked, putting his arm around her shoulders.

"I was talking to Elijah about when he was a slave, and …" Her throat tightened so she couldn't talk. She looked up into her father's eyes and burst into tears. He held her tightly for a few minutes and then gently leaned her up straight.

"Rebekah, you know how we learn about *gelassenheit*, about submitting to God, and treating people with love even when they do you harm?" he quietly asked. She could only nod her head. "That's what makes us different. We don't mistreat people like Elijah just because he is different. That's not God's way. And we don't fight back when people treat us badly, either. Do you remember the story of Jesus saying that when someone hits you on the cheek, that you should turn the other cheek and let him hit you again?" Rebekah nodded again, still unable to talk. Turning his head to look down the street toward Cashtown, he said, "That's not how they live, and that is why we keep ourselves separate from them." She nodded, agreeing with him, at least for the moment.

With that, he snapped the reins and turned east on the pike, heading toward their farm. Rebekah was silent for the entire ride home. She was gaining a new appreciation of what it meant to be Amish, and yet … after her conversation with Elijah, the thought of slavery was more repugnant to her than ever, and she longed for an opportunity to do something about it.

On the other end of the wagon bench, Caleb Stutzman was deep in his own thoughts. He loved Rebekah so much! Thinking about Rebekah's spirit, and how strong her convictions about slavery were, he wondered if that conviction would pull her away from him and the Amish way of life. Blinking away his tears, he asked God to somehow end all the unrest before it took his precious child away.

Chapter Three
June 1863
The War Comes to Cashtown

When Rebekah turned thirteen in the early summer of 1863, she felt just as strongly as ever about slavery, and just as helpless to do anything about it as ever. She had no way of knowing that history was about to affect her life in a dramatic manner, and she was about to affect history in a way she never dreamed possible.

In late June 1863, the Pennsylvania countryside was abuzz with the frightful news that General Robert E. Lee and his Confederate Army of Northern Virginia were invading the North. People were uncertain about Lee's location and destination. They could only hope that the Federal Army of the Potomac would find and stop him before he and his Confederate army got to their own town.

Rebekah's mother, Emma, was frugal, a skilled cook famed for her shoofly pie, a talented seamstress, and the center of love in their large family. She was aware of the impending danger, thanks to the Amish grapevine.

"Mamm, where do you think General Lee is going?" Rebekah asked one morning in the kitchen after a trip to deliver eggs and vegetables to Mr. Mickley. The conversation she heard there alarmed her.

She'd noticed that while her father was unloading his wagon, Mr. Mickley had kept glancing up the Chambersburg Pike, where it came down South Mountain in front of his inn. A guest, standing nervously by him, said, "I don't think I am going to continue my trip to Chambersburg. I suspect Bobby Lee is on his way there now."

"I don't blame you, that's as good a guess as anyone has," Mr. Mickley replied. "It doesn't seem like even our own army knows where he is!"

Rebekah asked Mr. Mickley where Elijah was, since Mr. Mickley himself was helping her father unload the wagon. He had turned to take a wary look at the guest and said, "He went to work for my cousin in Boston for a while. He'll be back when all this mess is over."

Emma Stutzman, startled at her child's knowledge of General Lee and the war, shot back, "It's not for us to—" Then, after pausing to regain her composure, she said, "Rebekah, Liebchen, please draw another pail of water from the well." It was her mother's way of telling her that such a discussion was off limits.

On her way out the side door, Rebekah considered she might as well keep to herself her worries about what was happening. Her brothers, sisters, and friends knew or cared nothing about it, and her parents refused to even acknowledge to her that there was a war going on, and the frightful prospect of it was coming closer to their community. But she could certainly feel the mounting tension. Her mother and father were unusually quiet those days during meals. She imagined the prospect of the war terrified them, but they did not let their children know that. Rebekah herself said little at the table, lest she raise her parents' ire. But she worried about Elijah. Although a lot older than her, and not even Amish, she considered him a friend, and she was afraid for him. When she first heard Mr. Mickley say he had sent him away, she was upset that he'd done so. But as she thought about it more, she realized he'd probably sent him away to protect him, in case the Confederate army actually came this far north.

On June 26, what they all feared became all too real. Thousands of Confederate soldiers marched down South Mountain on the Chambersburg Pike and right through Cashtown on their way towards Gettysburg. The noise and dust of the approaching column of horses, cannons, creaking wagons, and soldiers on foot alerted the Stutzmans when the approaching army was still several miles off. Caleb quickly gathered his family and directed them down the narrow steps to the basement. There in the damp darkness, they listened as Confederate General Jubal Early's entire division marched down the Chambersburg Pike right in front of their home. In hushed silence, they heard the hoofbeats of hundreds of horses, followed by a seemingly endless sound of marching soldiers. The clanging of rifles and equipment gripped the Stutzmans in fear. In the barn and pastures across the road, the din frightened the farm animals, who voiced their fears in a cacophony of clucking, mooing, and whinnying as the sounds, sights, and smells of a hot army on the march enveloped the farm.

Fortunately, Jubal Early was eager to get to Gettysburg and kept his troops on a steady march, even where the Pike narrowed as it crossed Marsh Creek a little farther on. Only after the last sounds of the wagons at the end of the column had faded into the far distance did Caleb Stutzman venture up the stairs, after signaling to his family to remain in the basement. Slowly stepping onto the front porch, he looked up and down the Pike for any Confederates. A dust cloud to the east was the only sign of them. But the scattered dust, horse manure, and ruts in the road left no doubt that thousands of men and hundreds of horses had passed this way. Caleb looked with trepidation across the road, wondering if the Confederate troops had taken any of his animals. But other than the anxious sounds of the animals, all seemed well.

Turning back into his house, he tried to call down to his family that it was safe to come up from the basement, but was shocked to find he had lost his voice. The fear that had gripped him now made his throat so tight he could not talk. Swallowing, then breathing deeply for a moment, he finally told his family it was safe.

The next few days were quiet, but extremely stressful. Caleb told his children not to leave the property and to stay within sight. They carried out their daily chores as usual, but always keeping a wary eye and cocked ear, listening for the sound of more troops. Wanting to know more but realizing that his Amish friends might be as much in the dark as he was, Caleb ventured over to one of his English neighbors and asked if they still needed to be concerned. The look on the man's face gave him a simple answer, long before the neighbor explained that Robert E. Lee and the rest of the Confederate army were in Pennsylvania, but no one knew their location. Lee had to be forced back to Virginia before people could feel safe. An eerie silence had descended over Chambersburg Pike, normally a very busy road at this time of year, like the calm before the storm.

JUNE 29, 1863
Working Under the Clouds of War

After a tense and silent breakfast, Emma Stutzman instructed her children to go out to one of the many nearby blackberry patches and pick a pail each, so that she could boil them into preserves that afternoon.

"But don't stray too far," she warned.

"I won't. I'll just go over to the Yoders'," Ezekiel announced.

"No, you won't, child!" she shot back. "You'll stay on our farm."

The boys were growing up, Rebekah thought, as Ezekiel nodded obediently and headed out the door. He quickly agreed to follow his mother's instructions, so hopefully he wouldn't have to chop wood after he finished picking berries.

As usual, Ruth and Mary went in one direction and Zeph and Zeke in another.

Fine with me, Rebekah thought. *I know where the best spot for berries is, anyway.* After crossing the road, she paused between the barn and the chicken coop. One of the new kittens had wandered out of the barn and was chasing chicks around in the weeds at the edge of the chicken coop. She smiled and laughed at the sport of it.

"What would happen first?" she wondered. "Will the mother hen catch the kitten with her sharp talons and beak, or will Daed catch me just watching his prize chickens being disturbed, doing nothing and be angry with me?" Neither thought was a pleasant one, so with one hand holding up her skirt, she ran and swooped up the unsuspecting little cat with the other hand, then herded the straying chicks back to the mother hen inside the safety of the coop.

"You naughty kitten," she half scolded and half laughed at him. "That old hen will teach you yet to leave her peeps alone." She rubbed her nose against his wet nose while scratching him behind his ear. The kitten purred as she strolled into the barn to fetch an empty pail.

We are a lot alike; she thought. *We get into trouble trying to learn too much, too fast. And even though we both come from large families, we're alone a lot, too."* As soon as she placed him down in the barn's corner where the rest of his brothers and sisters were lying lazily in straw, the kitten turned and ran immediately back out the open door.

"Well, I warned you," she said with a smile as she headed toward Marsh Creek, to the low ground behind the barn. The creek was just off the edge of their farm, running through a wet bottom land that was too wet and muddy to plow. The farmer on the opposite side of Marsh Creek, not an Amish family, owned the land but used it only for hay and occasional grazing. Her feet sank into the soft ground as she approached the creek, but she nimbly moved through the thorns and weeds to find the best berry patches.

Marsh Creek is lonely and I'll never get in trouble here, she thought to herself. *If only the flies weren't so bad here!* Working her way into the prickly berry patch was difficult for her in her long skirt, but once she had made it into the middle, picking a pail full of ripe, juicy blackberries was easy enough.

The others are probably only half done, she mused as she set her pail down on the bank of the creek. She had plenty of time to rest, get a drink, and dangle her toes in the cool water before heading home. The hot, dry summer was taking its toll on the stream. A rushing torrent in April, the water was now only a few inches deep. She slipped her high shoes off and dipped her hot feet in the cool stream.

It was at that moment that horsemen approached from the west. She heard them first, the horse's hooves splashing as they rode right down the middle of the creek! Everything about the horses was fearsome: their long, shining legs; their large, sweating necks; and most of all, their gray-uniformed riders! Four horses, four men. But to Rebekah, they might as well have been Robert E. Lee and the entire Confederate Army! She stood motionless as they rode up to her. The first rider raised his right hand and stopped, and the others immediately stopped behind him.

He looked down at her. Her mouth was dry, and her legs were shaking. *What do they want? What will they do to me?* Her mind raced as he reached into his pocket and unfolded a crumpled piece of paper. It appeared to be a map.

"Is this Marsh Creek, Miss?"

She understood the words all right, but he talked differently than anybody she had ever talked to, and, besides, he called her "Miss," which was new to her.

"Is this Marsh Creek?" he repeated, a little louder and without the "Miss." She figured that meant he was getting mad, so she meekly nodded that it was.

He looked at his map again and, looking up toward her farm, asked, "Is that the Chambersburg Pike up there on the other side of that barn?" She nodded yes again. He put the paper back in his pocket. He nudged his horse forward, turning to the men behind him, and said, "Let's try to find that bridge." The others followed, constantly looking around. Up close, she noted, the men did not look so dreadful. The last one even smiled at her and said, "You better git home."

She waited until they disappeared around the bend and decided that she would do exactly that! Halfway out of the thicket, she remembered the pail of berries beside the creek.

"No sense getting in more trouble than I'm already in!" she said aloud to no one in particular. Turning around, she fought her way back through the thorns, picked up her pail, and ran. As she jumped over a fallen tree in the brush, her skirt caught on a branch and she tumbled onto the muddy ground, spilling the berries in the process. The heat of the day, the four horsemen, the prospect of getting into trouble for being off the farm, and now the sight of her pail lying on edge with blackberries strewn about was too much for her to handle. She burst into tears. Only the thought that the longer she tarried, the more trouble she would be in made her move again. Quickly, she turned the bucket upright and nuzzled as many berries as she could back into the pail. Next, she picked up as many berries off the ground as she could without smashing them.

"No problem," she thought. "I'll fill this to the top in no time flat." She was herself again. Her quick, nimble fingers reached among the thorny branches to pluck only the biggest, ripe berries, moving deftly from one bush to another. Her balance allowed her to reach berries deep inside the thorny bushes. In a few minutes, she was on her way again with a full bucket of blackberries.

"Mamm! Daed!" she shouted as she ran up from behind the barn. "Mamm! Daed!" Her mother came out to the porch as she ran across the road. Her father jumped down from the ladder he was using to hang the freshly painted shutters back onto the house.

"*Was ist los? Was ist los?*" he asked anxiously. *What's the matter?*

It wasn't at all like his dependable youngest daughter coming running across the barnyard screaming at the top of her lungs; something must be dreadfully wrong.

"Horsemen, four horsemen!" she gasped, holding up her hand with four fingers pointing up. "Four *Confederate* horsemen!"

"Where?"

Rebekah turned and pointed behind the barn, "In Marsh Creek, riding toward the bridge!"

"Stay here, get inside!" he ordered. "I'll get the others."

Her mother grabbed her hand and took her into the house. Rebekah now worried she would be asked what she was doing by Marsh Creek, after being told explicitly to stay on the farm. But Emma Stutzman didn't seem to care about that now.

"Are the boys back yet?" Caleb asked as he burst through the kitchen door with a frightened girl's hand in each of his. Ruth and Mary ran to their mother's side.

"No, not yet" Emma said.

"Where might they have gone?" he asked, rattled. After three girls, the boys were a well-received gift from God to an Amish farmer, and at times like these, he feared the worst.

"They're probably down by the old springhouse," Rebekah offered.

"There's precious few blackberries down there, child," he retorted.

"I know," she said, adding reluctantly, "but there is a good branch to swing from there." She didn't want to get the boys in trouble, but she truly was concerned for them.

Caleb charged out the door again in search of his errant sons.

A pillar of calm strength, Emma Stutzman put the girls to work, washing and crushing the berries in a big pot to be put on the woodstove. "Hard work solves most anything," she said, as she often did. "Hard work and prayer."

The sounds of cleansing water splashing over berries, split wood being thrown into the stove, and the pot beginning to bubble were all they heard as they worked together, silently praying for the safety of their missing sons and brothers. When they heard their father's voice just outside the house, they rushed out the door all at once.

"And tomorrow you will split two cords of wood! Now get inside," Caleb Stutzman bellowed as he hurried the boys up the front steps onto the porch, dragging a boy's ear in each hand.

Turning to Rebekah, he added with a sigh: "Rebekah, please clean the weeds and bugs off of their half-full pails before you bring them in the house." The pails had been set down at the bottom of the porch steps, and one had tipped, letting berries spill out. She slowly emptied one half pail into the other, stopping to fish out the odd bug or leaf the boys had carelessly picked up with the berries.

As she turned back towards the front door, Rebekah glanced past the barn, toward Marsh Creek. There was no sign of anything there, but up the Chambersburg Pike toward the Cashtown Inn and South

Mountain, she saw clouds of dust stretching far back to the west—ominous clouds of dust, the dust of thousands of men, with all their wagons, cannons, and horses. She didn't know it yet, but it was the dust of the leading edge of Confederate General A.P. Hill and the Third Corps of the Army of Northern Virginia.

On the front porch of the Stutzman farmhouse, Caleb instinctively stepped toward the approaching dust cloud. Looking up, Rebekah saw him thinking. He wasn't panicking, but she sensed his concern. Turning and looking east down the Pike toward Gettysburg, he asked Rebekah, without taking his eyes off the road, "Is that the way the horsemen headed?"

"Yes, they said they were looking for a bridge."

"The arched stone bridge, where the Pike crosses Marsh Creek," he reasoned. "They aren't far."

A moment later, he said: "Get the horses out of the pasture and into the barn. I'll get the cows and pigs. Zephaniah and Ezekiel, you get the two old cows wandering in back of the garden," he said, pointing to the rear of the house. Like many farmers, he often turned the older, slower cows loose to graze wherever they wanted, which ended up being where the grass was tall and green.

Turning to Rebekah again, he instructed her in a lower, more ominous tone, "Please be especially careful with Thunder." Even an English farmer might wonder why he was asking one of his daughters to get the horses instead of his sons, who were now ten and nine. But time was of the essence, and Caleb figured everything on the farm, everything he had worked so hard for, was threatened by the approaching army. Rebekah was still far better with the animals than his sons were.

"Emma, see if you can find some place to hide some of the food. We don't know that the army won't confiscate our stores to feed their hungry men. Mary and Ruth, work with your Mamm. Go now!" The Stutzman family moved quickly, each with a knot in their stomachs, but intent on doing what they needed to do and doing it quickly.

Rebekah strode across the road, looking carefully in each direction in case the horsemen had reappeared. Seeing none, she entered the pasture. The Stutzman's had six horses: four older plow horses, a newly purchased young filly, and two-year-old Thunder. They hadn't called him Thunder at first, but when he turned two, the big, spirited horse developed a habit when startled of rising on two legs and crashing back to the ground, making a sound like thunder. Rebekah would deal with him last. The plow horses were no problem, although she noticed they seemed to be more skittish than usual. Perhaps they smelled strange horses or were just responding to Rebekah's anxiety. She knew horses were keenly aware of the emotions of their human handlers and so made it a point to move deliberately, but not too quickly, so they would feel at ease. She smiled at them as she bridled them and led them into the barn one by one. The foal seemed unaware of any fear. At first, she ran away and darted back and forth across the pasture, but soon she responded to Rebekah's smile and soft voice. Rebekah caressed her nose and delicately slipped the harness on her. Once she had the filly in the barn, Rebekah felt her stomach tighten. Thunder would not go so easily.

She stopped by the springhouse and grabbed one of the last apples from last year's crop. Glancing up toward the road, she noticed that the dust cloud was getting larger … and closer. This made her feel anxious, but she tried hard to hide it from Thunder.

Out of the corner of her eye, she noticed the boys leading the two older cows across the road and into the barn. Her father had already put the rest of the cows into the barn and was working on getting the pigs inside. When the boys came out of the barn, they started to walk toward her. She loved her brothers, and for all their faults, she truly believed they were becoming good Amish farmers. But now was not the time to teach them about horses. "Go help Daed with the pigs," she said with a forced smile, never taking her eyes off of Thunder. When they continued ambling toward her, she hissed in as stern a voice as she could muster: "Now!"

Zephaniah and Ezekiel were getting more confident with age, but Rebekah had always commanded a certain respect from them, even more so than her older sisters. And they acknowledged she was much better with animals than they were. Suddenly, taking notice of the growing dust cloud down the road, they stopped in their tracks and then turned back toward their Daed, who was herding the previously penned pigs towards the barn.

Turning back to Thunder at the pasture fence, Rebekah smiled and waited for the boys to get around the barn and out of his sight. "Come on, boy, settle down." The apple she carried was old, and she felt the softness of rot in it. But an apple was an apple, and Thunder, like most horses, enjoyed an apple. Moving slowly toward him, she held it out. The effect was better than she had hoped. Thunder snorted and moved to Rebekah as she entered the pasture. "There you go!" she calmly told him as she gave him the apple. After chewing and swallowing it, he snorted several times, and she noticed his nostrils were no longer flaring. Nudging her, he almost welcomed the bridle as she slipped it on him. Perhaps he sensed the approaching danger and yearned for the safety of the barn, or perhaps it was just the effect Rebekah had on him. Leading him inside the barn and into a stall, she rubbed his nose and soothed him with her voice.

Rebekah had never liked pigs and felt no obligation to help get them in the barn. Her Daed and the boys were doing fine, anyway. Once all the animals were secure inside the barn, the four of them walked in silence across the Pike to their house. The low vibration of marching men and horses was audible now. Believing that they had done everything they could in the short time available, Caleb led his children into the front room of the house.

The family stood and looked at him in silence. No one knew quite what to do. Caleb stroked his beard as he looked at each of them and said, "Children, let us pray." Standing in a circle, they bowed their heads while he led a brief prayer in Pennsylvania German, asking for God's protection and the courage to remain peaceful, *nonresistant*, in the

Amish way, in the face of evil in this world. "Amen," the family chorused.

"Okay, we have a lot of berries," Emma said. "Let's finish making our jam."

"I'll fetch some water," Caleb said.

That statement shocked Rebekah. It occurred to her she had never seen her father get water. For as long as she could remember, that was a chore for one of the children. He obviously did not want any of his children to venture outside, even the few steps from the side porch to the well. Nor did she remember him ever working inside the house when the weather allowed him to work in the barn or outside.

As it was particularly hot on this next-to-last day of June in 1863, the heat from the stove made the kitchen extremely uncomfortable.

"I wish I could go out on the porch to cool off," Zeke sighed.

"Or go to the well and get a cool drink," Zeph added.

One raised-eyebrow glance from their father quickly eliminated either of those suggestions. Rebekah thought the boys should be glad that, between the two of them, they had only picked enough berries to barely fill a bucket, so the jam-making process went quicker than it would have if they had filled their buckets like Rebekah. Indeed, the jars of blackberry jam were full by late afternoon, and she carried them down into the basement. Rebekah noticed that most of the shelves were empty. While their stock of food was always low in early summer, before the new harvest came in, she knew they had more left than was on the shelves. Glancing toward the front wall of the basement, she noticed something was different. Toward the end of the shelves, the big rock was back in the wall. She smiled, thinking how smart her mother was. Since the front porch faced north and had a solid stone foundation, it was cool underneath. They sometimes put food in there if they wanted it to stay cooler than the rest of the basement. Her Mamm and her sisters had apparently moved a lot of their food stores to that spot under the porch before putting the stone back in place to hide it. She'd left just enough jars on the shelves to avoid suspicion.

Upstairs, the pails were washed, and the kitchen stood spotless. Spotless, that is, except for a pot of leftover chicken soup being warmed for supper. Soup and bread would be all today, the children realized, as their Daed would let no one venture to the chicken coop for a chicken or to the garden for some fresh vegetables.

Chapter Four
June 29, 1863, Evening
A Good House for a Headquarters

It was a strange scene. For an Amish farmhouse to be so still and quiet in the middle of a day that was not the Sabbath was unheard of. Tensely, the family waited, not understanding what to expect. The sounds of a horse coming from the direction of Gettysburg broke the silence. Instinctively, they moved toward the windows and saw a rider in gray stop in front of their porch. Rebekah recognized him as the lead rider of the men she had encountered earlier that day in Marsh Creek. After looking around him, he dismounted, tied his horse to the picket fence in front of their yard, and very deliberately walked up the stone walk and then up the five steps to their front porch. They all looked to their father, who, upon the man's firm knock on the door, moved to open it.

"Lieutenant Samuel Barker, 26th North Carolina," said the Confederate standing on the front porch.

That same strange way of talk, Rebekah thought as she remembered her frightening encounter with the four horsemen, which seemed like weeks ago instead of just a few hours. But as he asked her Daed questions and he answered, she realized how peculiar Daed must sound to the officer. Her mind couldn't help but wonder how big the world really was.

"We are going to need your house and your farm." The soldier said it politely but sternly. He was not asking; he was telling them. Caleb looked at him, not understanding what he said, or as Rebekah thought, not wanting to understand.

"What?" Daed asked softly in their German dialect.

"We will pay you in Confederate money, don't worry." But how could the family not be worried? Looking around the home, the Lieutenant was nodding his head appreciatively. "This will make a good headquarters. I'm gonna need y'all to stay upstairs while we are here," he politely but firmly instructed them.

The Stutzman house really was a fine home, standing out even among the sturdy homes of the other farmers in this fertile part of central Pennsylvania. Five wide steps led up to a covered front porch that ran the entire length of the house. The house was faced with stone hauled up from Marsh Creek. Rebekah's mind slipped back to the summer when she was eight years old. Her Daed had just finished repairing the framework of the house, which had been run down when they moved in, and her mother suggested they just finish it in wood siding like many other homes. But Caleb Stutzman wanted a stone house, and he had a problem. The section of Marsh Creek where there was a lot of stone was difficult to access. In order to bring a load of stone up the sharply angled rise from the creek bed, one person was needed to steer the wagon from the seat of the wagon, and another was needed to lead the team by pulling their bridle. Rebekah's mother was busy with the young boys, and her sisters were afraid of the cats, let alone the horses! Their Amish neighbors said they would be glad to help after the harvest, but Caleb wanted the house completed before cold weather set in. Besides, his neighbors had already spent many days that July helping him repair the framework and nail on the new roof shingles. So, if the Stutzman house was going to have stonework on the outside, it would have to be accomplished within the family. Laying the stone was not a major problem; Caleb was an accomplished mason, trained by his father. The trouble was getting the stone from Marsh Creek to the house.

"Why don't you have Rebekah help, Daed? She likes animals so much anyhow," Ruth had said, just a bit sarcastically, one night at supper.

Mamm had sternly but calmly replied, "Working with a team of horses is for men, not eight-year-old girls. Now finish your supper in silence, Ruth."

However, Caleb was determined enough to have a stone house that he quietly considered this option. Rebekah had always been helpful with the animals.

"Do ya think ya can help me, Rebekah?" he ventured.

"I'll sure try, Daed!" she replied with a twinkle of eagerness in her eyes and try she did! They loaded the wagon together, and then Caleb would sit in the wagon to command the horses and steer the wagon. Rebekah walked in front, holding the bridles of the front two horses. She pulled and coaxed them up the steep bank and along the narrow, twisting path to the Pike.

His supply of river stones in place, Caleb started to lay the walls. But as Rebekah started to move stones in place for him to lay them, he sternly stopped her. "No, no, Rebekah, I'll do it." She could see the mixed emotions in his eyes as he motioned her away. He was extremely proud of his little girl but could not bring himself to set her to tasks never expected of a young Amish girl. It would not look good for their neighbors to see a little girl helping to lay stone.

In the years since then, the pattern continued. When her Daed needed help that no one else could provide, he called on Rebekah. These were special times for her, times she felt closer to him than she ever felt to anyone. But quickly, as the task at hand was completed, she would be sent back to the house to work with Mary and Ruth. They, in turn, typically picked the easier jobs and sent her to tend to the chickens or to work in the garden.

Now, with the boys being older, the special times with her Daed were fewer and fewer. Rebekah realized that her ability to help sometimes made it rough on Zeph and Zeke. In times of exasperation at their inability to handle a task, he would compare them unfavorably with her. When her father broke his leg that spring, the boys returned to their father's bedside one rainy evening to report that the cows were standing outside under the oak tree, refusing to come into the barn.

"Then get Rebekah to show ya how to do it!" he hollered. And she did show them, trying hard to be humble and not to show any pride in her abilities. Pride, she knew, was a sin that a good Amish Christian took pains to avoid.

The inside of the house the Confederate officer surveyed was a testament to the diligence and handiwork of the Amish women. Neatly embroidered drapery hung on all the windows. Stitched samplers featuring biblical verses decorated the walls. The main floor contained the kitchen, dining room, and a big main room. A large, open stairway led to an open loft where Rebekah's brothers slept, flanked by two bedrooms. The bedroom on the right was for the girls, and the left one for her parents. Handmade quilts, painstakingly stitched from squares of colorful fabric, covered each bed. Each bedroom had a large window looking out the side walls of the house.

The kitchen was the busiest and most important room in the house. Plain, simple cooking wares sat neatly and precisely stacked, each in its own place. The black wood-burning stove still had hot coals in it.

"Yes, this will make a good headquarters," Lieutenant Barker announced as he emerged from the kitchen. "Please have your entire family fed and moved to the upstairs rooms in one hour. We will reimburse you tomorrow. Thank you." With that, he turned and left the house.

As the family made their final preparations for bed, they heard dozens of soldiers setting up their tents in their fields. With wide, fearful eyes, Rebekah noticed the effects of the army descending on their farm. The vast piles of split and dried firewood the boys had stacked so neatly quickly disappeared into hundreds of campfires. A line formed in front of the chicken coop as chickens were caught, beheaded, and passed out to be cooked for supper. An enormous man with a stack of papers in his hand was in charge, constantly yelled out numbers and names like "Second Company only!" "One chicken for every two men!" and "Lieutenant Jenson's troops next!"

Rebekah searched her Daed's eyes for signs of anger, but she saw none. She admired his self-control. She knew how hard he had worked to build up the chicken flock. How they had taken eggs and chickens for themselves sparingly, and only sold what they needed to for cash. Rebekah Stutzman did not need to see human bloodshed to realize that war was terrible; she saw it as one regiment made camp on her farm.

The Stutzman family quickly finished and cleaned up after their supper, used the outhouse, and then climbed up the stairs to the second floor. Rebekah, looking out the window in the girl's room, on the side of the house toward Cashtown, noted that, although the road all the way back toward the Cashtown Inn was filled with soldiers and horses, the dust cloud was still rising from the side of South Mountain.

How many men could there be in this army? she wondered to herself with growing dread. Although she could not see the barn across the Pike from the side window, she could hear Thunder neighing in the barn. Her heart pounded as she worried the army might take him. The Stutzman could replace the food, but they needed excellent horses to run their farm in the future, and once they had him broken, Thunder would be a great lead horse for a team hitched to a plow or a wagon. Plus, Caleb was expecting him to sire many big, powerful horses in the years ahead.

Rebekah heard many men talking and working downstairs in the kitchen, and others who were sitting at the table. Knowing how much her father could eat after he had worked all day, she could not imagine how much food it would take to feed all these hungry men. She knew the fresh blackberry jam would be gone, and wondered how much other food people had taken from the basement. Lieutenant Barker interrupted her thoughts, stepping up the first few treads of the stairs. Stopping about halfway up, evidently to respect the family's privacy, he called out, "Sir!"

Moving toward the top of the stairs, Caleb Stutsman replied, "What is it?"

"Your big horse is spooking our horses. Someone needs to calm him down." As Caleb descended the stairs, Lieutenant Barker held up his hand and said, "No, not you. You must remain up here. Send one of your boys, please."

Caleb looked at the boys for a moment, and then turned to his younger daughter. "Rebekah, please settle Thunder."

For the first time that she could remember, Rebekah did not get a glowing feeling when her father picked her over her brothers to work with the animals. She did not know what walking onto the front porch, down the steps and across the road would be like with all these strange men around. But her father needed her to go to protect Thunder from harm, so she obediently got up and started down the stairs. As she passed her Daed, he put his hand on her shoulder, signaling her to stop. Looking at Lieutenant Barker, he asked in English, "Are you a father?"

"I have a one-year-old daughter,." Barker replied.

"*Gute.* Then you go with her and stay with her while she settles the horse." He was not asking; he was telling Barker to watch over his daughter, hoping that as a father himself, Barker would instinctively do what was necessary to protect Rebekah. As she walked down the stairs, she noticed that all the men in the house stopped what they were doing to look at her. It was the same when Barker led her onto the porch and across the Pike to the barn. Although she never looked at the men directly, she noticed that many were no older than her sisters, and some looked even younger. She had never paid much attention to boys, and until recently, boys paid very little attention to her, except for the Yoder brothers. But that spring, her Mamm had sat her down and told her that since she was growing up, and growing out, things would be different for her when she was around boys. She could sense the men looking at her.

A powerful urge came over her to turn and run back to the house and back up the stairs into her father's arms. But her father expected her to protect his prize horse, and she intended to do just that.

As they walked down the side of the barn toward the doors in the back, Thunder's whinnies grew louder and more urgent. As Lieutenant

Barker led her around the rear corner of the barn, he suddenly ran ahead into the barn, and shouted, "Stop!" A step behind, Rebekah saw two young soldiers trying to harness Thunder, who was having none of it. "Leave him alone! I told you not to touch the horses!" Barker shouted. "These people will need them to take in the harvest after we have left."

"Yes, sir," they both replied sheepishly and then quickly disappeared out the door. Thunder was still neighing, slamming his shoulders against the sides of his stall and stomping his feet. Behind the barn, Rebekah heard the Confederate horses in the paddock running, snorting, and neighing in response. She realized why the Confederates had demanded they calm Thunder; he was spooking their horses when they needed to be resting. Reaching up her hand and soothing Thunder, she quietly whispered, "Shhhh, shhhh." Thunder snorted, shaking his head back and forth. Then, taking a step forward, he lowered his head and nuzzled her hand. "It's okay, shhhh." She smiled at him while patting his neck.

Without taking her eyes away from Thunder, she asked in the English she had learned at school, "Do you have horses at home, Lieutenant?"

Lieutenant Barker, standing about ten feet behind her, replied, "Sure, but I will say that none is as fine as this one here. I come from Ashe County, North Carolina. It's hilly, and we don't have fields this rich and flat, either." Looking around, he added, "or barns this big." He had heard many comments from his men about how big the barns were in Pennsylvania and how fat the animals were.

"How many slaves do you have?" Rebekah asked. She thought he might consider that an inappropriate question, but since he was from North Carolina, which she knew was in the South, she pictured Amos, Hannah and Moses as his slaves.

"I ain't got no slaves. We got very few in Ashe County. They're mostly down on toward the tidewater."

She sensed he was somewhat perturbed at being asked such a question, but she could not keep herself from continuing, "Then what are you fighting for?"

"We're fighting for our rats," he replied.

With a look of surprise and disbelief, she turned and looked at him. "We don't have any rats here, ever since Daed got that big yellow cat."

"Not *rats*," he snapped back in an elevated whisper, so as not to agitate the horse. "Rights! We are fighting for our *rights!*" He drew out the word "rights" so she could understand what he said. He certainly did not feel he owed this impertinent girl an answer at all, but he wanted people in the North to understand what this war was about from the South's perspective. He felt like putting her in her place, but she had settled down the big horse somewhat, and for that Barker was thankful. Plus, he understood enough about the Amish to realize that they were not involved with the federal government, let alone the Yankee army.

Knowing she absolutely should let it go, but feeling unable to do it, Rebekah said in a quiet, soft, but somewhat accusatory tone, "You mean you are fighting for the right to own slaves."

Lieutenant Barker's face flushed red, but he decided there was no point in arguing the point with someone as unimportant as Rebekah. Plus, calming the Confederate horses so they could rest was the most important thing to him right then. The horses had been ridden hard for days, and he knew they would likely be ridden hard again tomorrow. Their well-being was important, especially the well-being of his own horse. He knew that the federal government provided horses for the Union Army, but in the Confederate Army, cavalrymen and scouts were required to supply their own. Since he owned a horse, his regiment assigned him to scout for them, even though he wasn't part of a cavalry unit. He and his men moved ahead of the infantry, finding roads and locating the enemy. It was dangerous, but he did not want to fight on his feet shoulder to shoulder with the infantry. Far too often, he had seen them cut down mercilessly by cannon and rifle fire. A few minutes passed in silence, with neither of them wanting to continue the argument.

Finally, Rebekah asked, "Can I just walk him around the barn for a minute? It will settle him down."

"What if he up and bolts?"

"He won't," Rebekah assured. "He just wants to let everyone know it is his barn."

Sighing, Barker reluctantly nodded. "Please don't let him take off."

With a slight smile, she instructed confidently, "Slowly open the stall door once I have him harnessed." Once out of his stall, Thunder's demeanor changed. He quietly let Rebekah lead him down the center aisle of the barn. At the far end, Rebekah reached into a bin built against the front stone wall of the barn and grabbed an ear of corn. It was last year's, so it was hard and dry. But Thunder bit half of it off when she offered it to him, and then, after some chewing, took the second half gently from her hand. "Good boy, Thunder, good boy."

Leading him back to his stall at the far end, she noticed that most of the pigs and cows were gone. Looking closer, she realized that only the milking mothers and their young were still in the stalls and pens. Just a few hours earlier, her brothers and father had brought all their livestock into the barn. She detected the sweet smell of roasting meat in the air, and she realized where the missing animals had gone. The Confederate army had spared the animals that her family would need to survive on, and for that, she was grateful. But she gave Barker a knowing stare of disapproval, anyway.

Immediately understanding her thoughts, he furrowed his brows and said in a slow but husky voice, "You shoulda seen what the Yankees did to the farms in Virginia!" Rebekah sensed she was in no position to argue, and she led Thunder back to his stall. Removing the harness, she rubbed the side of his head and assured him, "You're okay, big boy, you're all right."

As they exited the barn, Rebekah noted that the army horses were quiet now, feasting on the lush green grass. Thunder had truly been the source of their anxiety. When she and Barker came up to the front corner of the barn and started heading towards the road, she overheard a soldier say as he looked down the road toward Cashtown, "Here comes the Boy Colonel." That got Lieutenant Barker's attention, and he stopped at the edge of the road, putting his arm in front of Rebekah to signal her to stop and stand by his side. He waited for several men on horseback to ride up. In the lead was a young man who carried himself with an air of importance, in a uniform that seemed more elegant than those of the rest of the men. As he pulled his horse to a stop in front of Barker, they saluted and Barker greeted him respectfully: "Good evening, Colonel Burgwyn!" Motioning toward the house, he said, "This is our headquarters tonight."

Eyeing up the house, scanning the men eating around campfires in the nearby fields, he replied, with a slight smile, "Good choice, Lieutenant Barker." Turning to Rebekah, the Colonel tensed and asked, "Who is she?"

"She's just a little Amish girl," Barker replied. "I needed her to calm down their horse in the barn."

This seemed to satisfy the Colonel, who now looked down the Pike toward Gettysburg and asked, "Do you have pickets up?"

Rebekah did not understand why the Colonel was talking about putting a picket fence up when the Confederate army appeared to have torn down most of their fences for firewood, but she wisely kept her thoughts to herself.

"Yes sir!" Turning his shoulders and pointing to the lower land behind the barn, he added, "There is a good-sized creek called Marsh Creek running in those lowlands, and it turns and crosses this road about a mile or so up there." He pointed towards Gettysburg. "There is an arched stone bridge where the road crosses the creek. The road leads into a good-sized town straight ahead called Gettysburg, about five miles away. I have an entire company guarding the bridge."

Nodding approval, the Colonel, who was still astride his horse, said, "Good work, Lieutenant. Now let's have supper. General Hill and General Pettigrew are going to be up to look around in a bit."

With that, he dismounted, handed the reins of his horse to one man whom he had ridden in with and followed Lieutenant Barker up the front walk. When she realized they were heading into her house,

Rebekah hurried ahead, taking the steps to the front porch two at a time, and running through the front door. She was halfway up the stairs to the second floor by the time the officers came in.

Without saying a word, she nestled in to sit between her Daed and Mamm on the boys' bed. Daed gave her a relieved look, and Mamm held her hand. They could hear the officers below sitting down at their dining room table to eat. After all the chairs slid up to the table, the talking stopped. She heard the colonel, the man referred to as the Boy Colonel, say, "Lieutenant, would you be so good as to say the grace?"

"Yes sir," Lieutenant Barker replied, then after a pause, prayed in a voice loud enough to be heard upstairs. "God in Heaven, we thank thee for this day, for this food and for blessing us in thy work. Watch over us in these difficult times. In the name of Jesus, Amen." Although she didn't remember any meal at that table starting without a prayer, hearing the Confederates pray seemed strange to Rebekah, and not only because it was in English and not her familiar language of prayer. Their way of speaking English was so different from anything she had heard before. But even more strange was how they could they pray to the same God as her family when people where they came from owned slaves. Like the wicked pharaohs of Egypt! Okay, she told herself, maybe all these men did not own slaves themselves. After all, Lieutenant Barker had told her he did not. But that was what they were fighting for! That was what this terrible war was about. Barker had told her it was for their *rights*. But with a touch of forbidden pride, Rebekah remembered how she had spoken more bluntly to him than she had spoken to any other grown-up in her life when she accused him of fighting for the right to own slaves.

At that moment, her father, perhaps sensing her tumultuous thoughts, pulled her tighter, as if to say: *Enough of that thinking; let them live in their world and we will live in ours.* As she looked around at her family, first at her Daed, then her Mamm, to her sisters Ruth and Mary, and finally to Zephaniah and Ezekiel, she mused that there was a lot of truth in what Daed had taught her, how he had raised them. "Godliness with contentment" was a phrase she had often heard at

Sunday meetings, and one her Mamm often quoted when someone complained about not having something.

The sounds of several horses riding in from the direction of Cashtown interrupted her thoughts. She heard the riders reining in their horses as they arrived at their house. Judging by the noise on the steps, there were four or five of them, and they walked through the front door together. Peering over the edge of the railing, Rebekah could see their heads as they strode in and then heard the dining room chairs slide back in unison and the men at the table stand up. There was a quiet moment when Rebekah realized they must have saluted, and then the older one said, "As you were. We don't want to spoil your supper. We just ate a big meal back at the Cashtown Inn. It took a long time for the owner to get us fed. Apparently, the owner just lost his cook, probably because he was drafted into the Federal army. But it's a real nice Inn and we will stay there tonight." Pausing a moment, evidently to glance up the stairs, he asked to no one in particular, "Who's up there?"

Lieutenant Barker replied, "Just the family that lives here. They are part of that Amish sect. They don't want nothing to do with his war, and they don't fight in it either. There are some more families like them around here, and a lot more to the east, as I understand."

"General Heth, is General Hill up yet?" asked the Boy Colonel.

"Not yet, Colonel Burgwyn. He should be soon. As far as I know, he is still in Chambersburg. So, Barker, what do we have in front of us?"

"Not much. We think we saw some militia in that town ahead, but we didn't get too close."

After a moment of silence punctuated by the sounds of clinking silverware as the men continued to eat, the man referred to as General Heth, who seemed in charge, said, "General Lee believes the Yankees are coming up a lot faster than we first thought. We believe they are about to complete their crossing of the Potomac and are moving quickly north. Most of them are already over the river. We're all spread out, which is dangerous with them getting so close. So General Lee wants us to consolidate here, at Cashtown. We'll have the high ground at our back, and if we must retreat, we can go back across the mountain to Chambersburg. The rest of General Heth's division will come over that mountain tomorrow. But I sure would like to know who is in that town ahead—what's the name of it again, General Pettigrew?"

"Gettysburg, sir."

General Heth replied, "Thank you, General Pettigrew. I want you to gather a group of men to ride into that town tomorrow and search for some supplies. We particularly need shoes."

Rebekah strained to listen to the discussion in the dining room below. The open stairs and some gaps in the floorboards allowed the men's voices to rise from the dining room. She noted a pause at this point. General Pettigrew seemed to be thinking about the orders to go to Gettysburg in the morning.

"General Heth, it was my understanding that General Lee's orders from last night were that we are not to bring on a large engagement until our entire army is consolidated. If there are Federal troops in Gettysburg other than local militia, we may get ourselves tangled up in a battle prematurely. Perhaps we should wait another day or two, or at least until General Hill arrives with the rest of the Third Corps, before we act rashly. Besides, I understand that General Early went through Gettysburg on the 26th. I expect that he would have gathered any shoes if they were available."

Detecting impatience in General Heth's voice, Rebekah heard him quickly shoot back, "General Pettigrew, this is my division, and I am ordering you to move towards Gettysburg in the morning." Pausing, apparently to look around the table, he said to all of them, "Now, we all know how the Yankees have ravaged Virginia the last couple of years. General Lee said we need to respect these people and pay for what we take, but we need supplies for our army." Pausing and turning back to General Pettigrew and lowering his voice, he added, "John, I am not telling you to start a battle. I just want you to go into that town and see what you can get."

Rebekah noticed that the other officers became quiet after that. General Heth changed the subject to one that caused Rebekah's heart to beat quicker.

"It has been reported that several hundred darkies have been rounded up and sent back South. They all claim to be free men, but y'all know how they lie!" This caused a chuckle among the other officers. Rebekah was horrified by the idea of black men being returned to slavery, and she prayed for Elijah's safety. She planned to thank Mr. Mickley personally for watching out for Elijah the next time she saw him. General Heth continued, "Gentlemen, we do not need to defeat the entire Yankee army; we only need to bloody them and bring the war successfully into Pennsylvania. If we can show these people that we are winning, and perhaps get England or France to back us, that will force Lincoln to stop this war of aggression and let us be."

With that, the men talked more casually, turning to discussions of their loved ones back home and how healthy the Pennsylvania farms were. They sounded like Amish farmers did when they gathered to talk about these subjects. That is, except for the discussion about slaves. From that perspective, Rebekah suddenly felt profoundly glad to be Amish, and not part of these worldly people with their evil ways. It was a tough life, but their entire community worked hard and they all shared the rewards. She imagined black men who had been free, now being captured, whipped, and chained up so they could be shipped South into slavery. Her entire life, she had been taught that anger was a sin, but now she felt herself becoming very angry indeed.

As sunset, activity in the house and farm quieted down. The officers downstairs set up cots or rolled their bedrolls out on the floors. With the windows open on the second floor to catch the breeze and relieve the stifling heat, she could smell campfires and the scents of cooking food from the tent encampment in their fields. The rest of her family fell off to sleep, but Rebekah could not stop thinking about the people taken back into slavery. She thought about the pamphlet she had seen that day in Cashtown years ago, of Amos being whipped, Hannah crying, and Moses being sold away.

How could men do this? Even more troubling to her, how could men who prayed to and revered the same God as she and her family do this to other people? It made no sense to her. She thought about what the Confederate Lieutenant Barker had said in the barn earlier that afternoon, that he was fighting for his "rights." Well, who was fighting for the rights of the slaves? It must be the Federal Army. But they were nowhere around. She muttered quietly to herself, "What can I do, what can I do?" Feeling troubled and hopeless, she finally dozed off to sleep as a light rain fell.

Chapter Five
June 30, 1863
Living with the Enemy

Early the next morning, her father woke her. She had slept late, and the house was in a bustle. Lieutenant Barker was halfway up the stairs, waving the family down. "He is giving us a few minutes to go to the outhouse and get some water and food. Come on, Rebekah! It's not like you to sleep in. "

"I know, Daed, but I had a hard time going to sleep last night."

With a light hand on her shoulder, he replied softly, "We all did Rebekah. We all did."

Each member of the Stutzman family used the outhouse, took a long drink from the well and ate what was left of the officers' breakfast in their kitchen.

As the family was scurrying back up the stairs, she heard her father ask Lieutenant Barker, "What about my animals? Somebody needs to feed them, milk the cows, give them water." Lieutenant Barker looked down, not wanting to tell Caleb Stutzman how few animals he still had.

"Send the girl and the two boys over to the barn. But hurry, I must leave soon."

Caleb looked at Rebekah and nodded, signaling her to go. She was confident she could make sure the animals were taken care of, and she was happy when her Daed gave her a slight, encouraging smile. Turning toward the front door, she grabbed her two reluctant brothers by the hand and said, "Hurry, we have to save whatever animals we can." She knew how much of their precious livestock had been taken the night before, and wondered how much more would be butchered today.

Barker led them quickly across the road and into the barn, trying not to call attention to them. The soldiers were busy getting ready for their day and didn't take notice. She fed the few animals that were left, making sure Thunder had a full trough. The last thing she needed was for him to get hungry and start acting out again. The Confederates might just kill him if he caused more havoc with their horses.

"Clean out the manure," she quietly commanded her brothers. Realizing after a few moments that they had not moved, she turned and pulled hard on Zephaniah's ear. He was almost as tall as her now and already heavier, but he still feared her because of how tough she had been on him when he was younger. Plus, he had to respect her because of the confidence their Daed placed in her. He grabbed a shovel, and Zeke grabbed a pitchfork, and they started to clean out the manure.

Rebekah remembered her Mamm had just recently pointed out that soon the boys would be bigger than her, and a lot stronger. She often repeated to Rebekah, "Amish girls don't boss boys around." Rebekah knew the day would come when she couldn't push them around like this, but today wasn't the day. With one eye on the boys and another on the door, watching for any Confederates who might come in, she got the few remaining animals fed and watered and the cows milked.

"Stay close to me," she instructed her brothers as she led them out the back door. But as they came around the corner of the barn, she abruptly stopped and reached for their hands. The road was filled with line after line of Confederate soldiers! She heard their horses stomping the ground, neighing and snorting, and the sound of metal on metal from the officers' sabers and the soldiers' guns. It was downright frightening. Her heart thumped as she noticed all the soldiers looking at her as she and her brothers walked up the hill toward the Pike. Remembering what her Mamm had told her about how boys would look at her differently now that she was maturing, Rebekah kept her eyes fixed on Lieutenant Barker. Stopping a few feet from the lines of soldiers, she stood erect, but intensely aware of every curve in her body, she sub-consciously pulled each of the boys in front of her to shield her from the gazes of the Confederate soldiers. Barker was on his horse right in front of her, talking to the man they had referred to as the Boy Colonel the day before. His head was turned toward Colonel Burgwyn, so he did not notice her and her brothers coming up toward the road from the back of the barn.

"What are we waiting for, Colonel Burgwyn?" Barker asked.

"Pettigrew wants to take a few cannons, just in case."

Barker looked perplexed. "I thought all they had in that town was some militia, and besides, aren't we supposed to avoid a battle?"

Burgwyn looked straight ahead and quietly, tensely replied, "General Pettigrew is not so sure there isn't more than just militia in Gettysburg."

At that moment, Barker noticed Rebekah. She had one hand on Zephaniah's shoulder and the other on Ezekiel's. Turning back to his men standing in the road, he commanded, "Soldiers, make a gap right here!" The men immediately complied, and she led the boys safely across the road and up the front porch. Turning, she noticed Barker was still looking at her.

"Git back upstairs and stay there," he instructed. "I must leave for a while." With that, he rode forward, and she noticed that the column of men came alive all at once, moving forward quickly. It was a spectacular sight—all these men marching off at once, a few of them whooping and hollering. The officers rode ahead, gazing intently at the road and the farms on either side. In the rear, three cannons mounted on wagons were pulled by six horses each.

Safely back inside her front door, Rebekah felt the heat and bustle of the kitchen as several men who were only partially in uniform were busy taking advantage of Mamm's very functional kitchen. She realized they were cooking for hundreds of men and had added most of the food Mamm had left on the open basement shelves to the supplies they had brought with them. Rebekah prayed silently that they had not discovered the food Mamm had hidden under the front porch.

Once up the stairs, she noticed her parents were in their room, looking out the window at the Chambersburg Pike as it stretched over the rolling hills toward Gettysburg. Noticing Rebekah peering behind them, Caleb turned and gave her a silent command to leave the room. Having seen that look many times, she immediately turned and walked out. She crossed the loft and entered the room she shared with her sisters. Looking out that window, she noticed that many of the soldiers remained in the tent camps on surrounding farms. Some were finishing their breakfast, while others were moving around from one place to another, a hive of activity. The further she looked back toward Cashtown, the smaller they appeared, like little gray ants, very busy gray ants.

Her parents had left their room and were sitting in the chairs in the loft, eating a cold lunch with their children and uneasily wondering when the troops would return. Rebekah asked to go into her parents' room to rest. But instead of lying down she went to the window and looked up the Chambersburg Pike toward Gettysburg. It was well past lunch when she first saw and then heard the soldiers returning from Gettysburg. They were not as loud or energetic as they had been when they left, but they did not seem overly tired, either. She knew that if they had gone as far as Gettysburg, they would have walked about ten miles altogether.

Toward the rear of the marching men, she noticed Lieutenant Barker riding his horse beside the colonel and the man she believed to be General Pettigrew. He was the one who had voiced his concerns last night at dinner about sending troops into Gettysburg. They were not talking much, but the general was frowning as if he was concerned about something. Rebekah looked over the edge of the side porch as they rode up to the side of the house. Dismounting, they tied their horses to the well so they could drink from a trough of water beside it. As they tended their horses, another group of horses could be heard clopping up the Pike from Cashtown. When they noticed General

Pettigrew standing by the well, the new group of riders turned and rode up to them.

"General Pettigrew, I am surprised to see you so soon. Did you get much in the way of supplies from the town?"

"No sir, General Heth!" Pettigrew replied. "Before we could get into the town, we spotted a column of Yankee cavalry moving up the road from south of town. We remembered General Lee's orders not to engage until our whole army is up, so we marched back." Glancing in the direction of Lieutenant Barker, he continued, "General Heth, Lieutenant Barker was scouting our right flank, and he believes he heard drums, so they may have some infantry coming up as well."

Looking back and forth at the three weary officers standing by the well, General Heth replied impatiently, "Gentlemen, surely you saw local militia! The Yankee army is not this far north yet!"

General Pettigrew, shaking his head, replied, "Sir, these men were cavalry. A lot of them were on horses and others had dismounted, but they were Yankee cavalry all right."

"General, we have encountered militia before, and this was not militia," Colonel Burgwyn added. "They carried themselves like soldiers."

As they talked, Rebekah stepped back from the window, far enough not to be seen but close enough to hear the officers' discussion. She noticed a young soldier walk over from the main group of tents and start to pump water out of the well into the trough. Lieutenant Barker immediately nodded at him, signaling him to leave the officers and go back to his men. Barker then grabbed the handle himself and pumped water into the trough. As one horse finished drinking, another immediately stuck its nose into the trough, nuzzling the other aside. They were hot and sweaty, and needed water.

As they continued their conversation, Rebekah heard yet another group of riders approaching from Cashtown, who also rode up to join the group by the well. The officers present silently saluted the leader of the newcomers. General Heth raised his head and said, "Welcome to

Cashtown, General Hill! I trust your ride over that mountain was fine, sir!"

Lowering his hand from the salute, the man referred to as General Hill dismounted, grabbed his horse's reins and led the animal to the trough. The others quickly grabbed their horses' reins and pulled them away from it. General Hill, dressed in a red shirt, stood out from the others in every way; he seemed a bit older and had a full beard. "I understand that we had some people in that Gettysburg town today?" he asked as he nodded up the Pike toward Gettysburg.

"Yes sir," General Heth replied. "General Pettigrew here took his North Carolinians, some Virginians and a few cannons toward that town this morning. He believes he saw some Yankee cavalry, sir, so he came back without entering the town. He did not want to violate General Lee's orders not to engage until the entire army is consolidated here.

Looking perplexed and irritated at the same time, General Hill replied, "I don't believe that! I just left General Lee in Chambersburg this morning and he doesn't think the main Yankee army is far above the Potomac yet. You must have seen militia, General Pettigrew."

Pettigrew was unwavering, even as Hill and Heth looked at him disapprovingly, as though he was mistaken and overreacting. Lowering his voice, but speaking confidently, he replied, "General, we saw cavalry in Gettysburg this morning, I am sure of it."

They all stood in silence for what seemed to be a full minute as General Hill gazed up the Chambersburg Pike toward Gettysburg. "No, they are not up yet. General Lee is certain of it."

Colonel Burgwyn, not wanting to take sides in the dispute but wanting to come to the truth, asked, "What has Jeb Stuart reported? Where does he perceive the Yankee army to be?"

At the sound of Stuart's name, General Hill sucked his breath in, and, with a tone of exasperation, replied, "General Lee has not heard from Stuart for days! He is telling us nothing. From what we read in the Yankee newspapers, he is riding all the way around the far side of the Union army, to the east of them. He hasn't told us anything about what we are getting ourselves into here. The newspapers are also telling us that General Meade is now in charge of their army, and Hooker is out."

Looking around at the others, General Pettigrew asked, "What do we know about him?"

"He'll fight!" General Hill responded. "General Lee does not believe he will move very fast, but he will fight when and wherever our armies meet. That's why General Lee now wants us to consolidate all our divisions, and pick good, high ground, and when General Meade comes up, he will have to attack us, on high ground of our choosing."

"Like Fredericksburg!" General Heth added.

"Like Fredericksburg!" they all said in chorus, with a smile on their faces.

After a moment of them all thinking about the place they called Fredericksburg, Rebekah noticed that General Hill was getting excited. "But we have time. The Yankee army isn't close yet. General Lee ordered Ewell to bring his troops back down from near Harrisburg, and he should arrive in Gettysburg sometime tomorrow. General Lee wants to consolidate our army there now. We will get all our divisions there before the Yankees and pick the ground!"

"Then you have no problem with me sending my entire division into Gettysburg in the morning?" General Heth asked.

General Hill took a moment to look at all of them and, with a confident smile, said, "None in the world!" With that, he reached for his horse and mounted. Looking at Pettigrew, he said, "I'm staying back at that Cashtown Inn with General Heth. It is a very fine inn. God be with you tomorrow! I will see you in Gettysburg in the next day or two!"

Rebekah sat down on the edge of her parents' bed. She played their conversations back and forth in her mind. She understood that the Confederate officers standing by her well had said that if they could get to Gettysburg before the Yankees, they could pick high ground and wait for this newly appointed General Meade to attack them. Since these men believed that the Yankees were heading toward Gettysburg, it was a race.

Then she remembered what she had heard the Confederates say the night before, that if they could win the next battle, they would win the war. And if that happened, the slaves would remain slaves. She remembered the story of Moses in the Bible, how God told him to go to that wicked pharaoh with one demand: *Set God's children free!* Surely the loving Father wouldn't want those poor people to be slaves any longer.

Shaking her head, her heart pounding, she whispered to herself, "That cannot happen, that cannot happen! The Yankees must get to Gettysburg first!" She also figured that since the Confederates didn't know where the Yankees were, it seemed logical that the Yankees didn't know where the Confederates were, either.

Then it came to her like a lightning bolt on a summer night: she would tell the Yankees where the Confederates are! She would sneak out, find the Yankee cavalry that she heard was in Gettysburg, and tell them where the Confederates were and where they were heading.

That it might be absurd to think she could do this did not enter her mind. It was simply what she had to do! She had heard many times at Sunday worship and from her Mamm that God has a purpose for all of us. *Well,* she said to herself, *maybe this is God's purpose for me. Maybe that's why I met that abolitionist in Cashtown.* If her Daed could leave his family behind in Lancaster and come here to build this prosperous farm out of nothing, then she could sneak out and walk the few miles to Gettysburg to free Amos, Hannah, and Moses.

Chapter Six
June 30, 1863, Evening
Rebekah Makes Her Move

The family was allowed to come down for a short time again before bed, but they were watched carefully. They used the outhouse and, gathering whatever food was left for them, they climbed the stairs again. Rebekah said, "Daed, I am going to sleep in the loft. It's cooler there."

They all lay down as the sun set, and before long everyone else had gone to sleep. All except Rebekah, who could think of nothing other than what she had decided to do that night.

"The Confederates must not get to Gettysburg first! They must not; I won't let them!" She thought it with such conviction that she actually said it aloud. A startled Zeph, who she thought was asleep beside her, mumbled, "What did you say?"

"Nothing, go back to sleep." The mere thought of doing anything at all gave her goose bumps. But once she was certain of what she was going to do, her sharp mind worked quickly. She knew that Marsh Creek turned flowed south after flowing under the Chambersburg Pike, and if she followed it, she believed that she would meet the Federal Army. In her mind, she pictured herself walking briskly through the creek as she had done many times before. It would be easy; she could do it! Then she looked down at the Confederate soldiers sprawled at the foot of the stairs and her heart sank. Marsh Creek might be easy to walk through, but that wouldn't matter if she couldn't get out of her own house!

So, she started to plan another way out. There was no way to get down the stairs with all the officers there, many of them still awake. Even if she could sneak down without anyone seeing her, there was a soldier on watch duty, marching back and forth across the front porch. There were about ten men sleeping virtually on top of each other in the kitchen, so she ruled that out. That left only the bedroom windows, which were fifteen feet above ground. She dismissed the idea of going through a window until she remembered the new kitchen porch her Daed had built on the left side of the house, facing the well. Sure! She could crawl out the window onto the new porch roof, lower herself onto the rail, and then jump to the ground. Just last fall, she had done basically the same thing when one of her kittens had been stranded on the porch roof.

But her heart sank when she remembered that Mamm and Daed were asleep in their bed, pushed against the window. Their heads were probably just a foot or so from the windowsill.

Rebekah thought again of the slaves. She must go! She forced herself to her feet to head to the bedroom.

"What's going on up there?" a soft but authoritative voice called up from below.

Her heart pounding, Rebekah turned, hoping he wasn't talking to her. But of course, he was. Everybody else upstairs was asleep.

"I'm just going to use the chamber pot," she replied. She sounded like a frightened little girl, and she certainly was a frightened little girl.

The soldier nodded, then turned away. When Rebekah returned to where she had been lying, she realized she would have to be more careful. She would have to plan every step, every move. The excuse of using the chamber pot had worked once, but it would be useless once she crawled out the window. She planned on twisting herself back to the door, like a snake in reverse. Then, while lying on the floor, she would reach up and turn the handle, opening the bedroom door just enough to crawl inside.

Her plan worked well until she realized that Zeph was sleeping too close to the door. She gently nudged his legs over. She had almost moved him far enough when he began to stir and rolled over, right beside the door.

"Boys!" she thought, "always getting in the way."

So, she moved him again, and when he seemed settled, she reached up and turned the doorknob, opening the door. The door creaked slightly, but after she was sure no one had heard anything, she crawled into her parents' bedroom, got to her feet, and closed the door quietly behind her.

As she turned to face the window, she saw Mamm propped up in bed, looking directly at her! She was caught. It was useless. No one ever talked his or her way out of anything with Mamm, not even Daed. So, she waited. She expected to hear her mother say, "Caleb, Caleb," and wake him up to handle the situation. But Rebekah heard nothing. Then, looking closer, she realized that her mother's eyes were closed in a deep sleep.

Rebekah gingerly walked over to the edge of the bed and, facing the window, leaned in over Mamm. Peering out into the darkness through the open window on this hot night, she could make out the porch roof only a few feet below. But how could she crawl over Mamm to get out of the window? She looked around and spotted a chair in the corner. Tiptoeing quietly, she picked it up and set it gently in place beside the bed.

Thinking her next steps over carefully, she looked out to see where the sentries were. She could still hear the footsteps of the soldier pacing the front porch. She noticed another walking around the house. She counted to about thirty-five before the sentry walking back and forth on the front porch returned to this side. It took about a count of fifty for the sentry circling the house to make each lap. She figured that if she waited until they both turned away at the same time, she would have about thirty-five seconds to get to the ground and get completely hidden in the shadows beneath the porch before they returned to that side of the house.

Standing up carefully onto the chair, she waited almost ten minutes for the timing to be right. When she saw her chance, she made her move. Putting her hands on the post at the corner of the headboard, she swung her right foot onto the windowsill. Leaning over the bed, she grabbed the bottom of the open window. She was extremely quiet, but she heard Daed start to make little snorts, as if a fly was on his nose. When she looked down, she realized the hem of her dress was swinging across his face.

If he wakes up now, he'll probably just throw me out the window before he realizes who it is, she worried. But he didn't wake up as Rebekah reached down and gathered the hem of her skirt with one hand while holding onto the window with the other.

No time to waste! She reminded herself, and, without waiting long enough to get scared, she balanced herself with her head out the window, feet together on the sill, and her arms above her holding onto the window. Then she jumped. The roof was a typical peaked roof, with the peak running away from the house. Her feet landed on the slopes to each side of the peak, slipping enough to make her lose her balance and smack her chin on the peak.

Ouch! She instinctively but silently mouthed. She got to her feet with her hand on the ridge and turned to check whether her parents had awoken. They had not, and the sentry on the front porch did not change his pattern.

"About twenty counts to go," she reminded herself. "No time to dally." She slid slowly down the roof on her right hip, holding on with her hands. At the bottom she put her right foot in the gutter, and with both hands holding fast, she swung her left leg over the edge, feeling blindly for the rail.

Only fifteen counts until the sentry turns. Oh! Where is the rail? Her heart was pounding. With her head facing directly into the gutter, she had no way of knowing now if she had been seen or not. Frantically, she swung her leg around midair, feeling for the rail. *It has to be there!* Then she remembered; Daed had built a step down off the kitchen door to the porch, but there was no step down from the front door to the front porch. So, if the side porch was a step lower, then so must be the rail on the side porch be lower as well. With a deep breath, she pulled her right foot out of the gutter and swung her leg through the air, with only her hands on the gutter. With a silent prayer, she let go. For an anxious moment, she was in a free fall, her feet falling to the rail she knew must be but a few inches below.

Clunk! The sound and feel of her feet landing squarely on the rail were a most welcome relief! Her next step was to grab the post at the end of the porch and lower herself to the porch, where she could easily walk down the steps and hide beneath it. But as she reached for the post with her left hand, something was holding her dress back! Knowing she was almost out of time, she instinctively yanked on her dress.

Come on! She pleaded. *Why won't it come free?* Then she saw her dress was caught on a nail that Daed hadn't completely set into the gutter. With time running out, she made a desperate move, jumping off the rail with her hands firmly clutching the dress.

"Please rip, please rip!" she prayed as she pushed her feet off the rail. Rip it did, with a noise that Rebekah thought would bring the entire Confederate army running right toward her.

She landed on all fours on the soft grass below, then scurried quickly back under the porch. Hugging the ground, she peeked out through the steps at the sentry, who was looking around the edge of the front porch toward her. He had heard the noise and was eyeing the side porch intently. A moment later, the other sentry came around the edge of the house at his normal pace, unaware of any noise.

"I heard something—check that side porch," the soldier on the front porch commanded. "What's that flapping in the wind, hanging from the gutter?"

The other sentry walked around the porch to the side from which Rebekah had just jumped? His boots were but half a step away from her face. If he bent over and checked under the porch, she would be caught.

Sometimes soldiers convince themselves there is danger in the night, even when there is none. At other times, when they expect a quiet, uneventful night, they have one because they fail to check out suspicious sounds adequately. The soldier whose feet stood inches from Rebekah's face was from Texas, and that was where his heart and mind were that bright June night.

"It's just a rag, hanging on the gutter to dry. Keep walking, Jeremy," he called as he turned and resumed his own casual march around the house. For five minutes, Rebekah didn't move or think. She just let her heart slow down. As best as she could make out, there was just the soldier marching back and forth across the front porch and the one marching around the house. But to her right, towards Gettysburg and Marsh Creek, there were hundreds of tents and dwindling campfires. She could not go that way, but what choice did she have?

For a few minutes more, she thought of various routes to get to Marsh Creek, and hopefully the Federal Army beyond. If she took a long route, she didn't stand much chance of getting there in time, so she would have to make it to the creek very soon. The plan she settled upon was to run across the Pike and slip behind the stump beside the chicken coop. She figured she could get there but not much further before the sentry on the front porch reached the far end and turned to march back. But he wasn't her only threat. She would have to start her run when both sentries were not looking in her direction.

She waited for what seemed forever for the right chance, but at least one of the sentries was always close to turning in her direction. What if she never got her chance? What if she spent the entire night waiting? What would she say in the morning when they found her hiding under the front porch?

"No," she demanded of herself; no matter how safe she was at this point, she would have to finish what she started. She counted every time the sentry circling the house disappeared behind the front porch. Sometimes she got to fifty by the time he got back around, but sometimes it was forty-six or forty-seven. But once she got past twenty-five, she knew that even if the other two were turned away, he would see her as he came around the corner of the house. She got to her hands and feet as the porch sentry approached the near end of the porch. She had only counted to twenty for the time the one circling the house was gone.

Okay, get ready, Rebekah, she encouraged herself as her heart began to beat heavily. Even though her plan was sound, it seemed much, much harder now that she had to do it.

Turn, turn, come on and turn! She pleaded in her mind to the sentry on the porch. But he did not turn! Not immediately, anyway, choosing instead to look back and forth over the yard. By the time he did turn, she had counted to thirty-two. That would make it entirely too risky. She lay back down and waited as the circling sentry reappeared at the count of forty-nine. The sweat on her brow now felt cold, but she knew she had made the correct decision to wait.

With every lap the sentries made, the chances of her getting through to the Federal Army were diminishing, especially with the moon coming up. Twice more, she got on her hands and knees to get ready to run when the situation looked good, and twice more, she lay back down as one of the sentries broke his pattern. Then she got her break. The sentry patrolling in front of her walked to the outhouse.

"I'll be a few minutes," he said to the soldier on the porch.

"Take your time," came the reply.

In about a minute, she had her chance. The sentry on the porch turned and headed back toward the far side of the porch. *I hope he stays in the outhouse a bit longer*, she prayed, and with that, she was off. She had always run fast, but tonight, she felt like she was gliding like a bird. As she approached the stump, she slid sideways behind it.

But the smooth landing she expected in the tall grass didn't happen. There were countless bumps on the ground, some quite pointy. Instinctively, she touched one. What was it? When she saw and felt that it was a chicken head, she let out a small shriek. Immediately she muzzled it by putting her shirtsleeve over her mouth.

I've blown it! I'm caught now! Rebekah cried in her heart. As she looked up, she saw the sentry come out of the outhouse and look directly toward her. She could see his silhouette clearly defined against the rising moon behind him. The fear of being caught, the pain of sliding on all the chicken beaks, and the sickening feeling of lying on all the blood and feathers nauseated her almost to the point of passing out. However, she heard no footsteps running toward her. She heard no voices.

Maybe they didn't see me, she hoped fervently. She pressed against the ground like a little child to her mother's skirt. She forced herself to remember her mission. "I must do it. I must help Amos, Hannah, and Moses. I'll have to get my strength back." But at that very moment, something brushed against her foot. Was it the musket of yet another sentry who came up from behind the barn? No, she realized, smiling, it was her favorite kitten. She reached for him and held him tight. With his purring, she felt stronger and braver.

I wish I could hold you and hug you all night long! She thought as she managed a thin smile. But she couldn't. Not now. She was committed. She must continue with her plan. The problem was that, until that moment, her plan had gone only as far as where she was now. She did not have a plan to get all the way to Marsh Creek.

Rebekah took stock of what she did know. She knew that Marsh Creek flowed in the same direction as the Pike before turning south and passing under the stone bridge. From what the Confederate generals had said, the Union troops were approaching the region around Gettysburg and Cashtown from the south. *Strange,* she thought, *the southern Confederate troops are to the north and the northern Yankee troops are to the south.* Just one more thing that she didn't understand about this war, but then again, that was just one more thing that she did not have to understand. What mattered to her was getting to Marsh Creek and walking downstream to somehow find some soldiers dressed in blue.

She turned slowly on her back and plotted a course down the hill beside the barn where she was now lying. She could see the low ditch where the water from the road drained when it rained. It was certainly low enough to conceal her, but walking through the tall cattails would give away her movements. No, that route wouldn't do. Perhaps she could crawl to the edge of the barn and disappear in its shadows. But she remembered the soldiers she had seen going into the barn before dark. She shuddered at the thought of being that close to so many of them.

She looked away from the barn and across the ditch to the fence line separating the pasture from the corn field. Just as she was set to begin crawling toward the fence, her heart once again became heavy. There was a sentry marching up and down the farm path between the fence and the cornfield! He would just about trip over her if she crawled down the side of the fence bordering the corn field. But the cows in the pasture on the other side of the fence had eaten all the weeds, so she would have nothing to hide behind. From where she lay, Rebekah pictured how easy it would be to notice a girl in a shiny clean dress. With a sudden resolve that surprised even her, she began to rub herself with chicken blood and guts until her simple, unadorned Amish dress was no longer so visible in the moonlight. Remembering her light brown hair, she grabbed two hands full of bloody dirt and slowly turned her hair dark. She even rubbed some of the disgusting slime on her face, careful to keep it away from her mouth. She found it strange to realize that she was actually doing all this, but then she remembered what her Daed had said when he began working before his broken leg was fully healed. "When times are tough, you do what you have to." And Rebekah Stutzman just had to get to Marsh Creek.

With her heart already pumping hard, her legs seemed to glide across the fifty feet of grass to the fence. When she reached it, she stealthily slid under it and then remained perfectly still for several minutes to make sure none of the soldiers had seen her.

Then, slowly lifting her head, she looked for the sentry coming up the path towards her. After spotting him and waiting to see him turn and go back down the path, she crawled behind him, on her side of the fence. When he again turned and marched back towards her, she stopped and lay perfectly still, with her face in the dirt, until he passed her. When he marched past, only a few feet from her, she wondered why he couldn't hear her heartbeat; it was so loud in her head. But he didn't, and in less than half an hour she had made it almost to where the fence ended, right before the tree line of Marsh Creek.

Rebekah was gaining confidence, almost to the point of getting careless. When the sentry turned and walked back up the hill, she got up on one knee and prepared to run for the trees and tangled weeds surrounding the water. At that very instant, she caught sight of another sentry coming toward her along the fence at the bottom of the pasture. She immediately dropped flat to the ground. *Has he seen me?* She shrieked silently to herself.

After a moment, she lifted her head ever so slightly to peek at the sentry. He was peering right at her! Once again burying her face in the dirt, she waited, almost certain he would come towards her. But there was only silence.

Rebekah made a contingency plan. If he came towards her, she would jump up and run for the trees. Hopefully, his gun wasn't ready to shoot, and she could disappear into the thicket. Then she would only have to worry about that General Stuart, who the officers in her house had said was riding around in the night. If the soldier's gun was ready to fire, then, well, she would be shot. Tears came to her eyes as the eerie silence continued.

Then the man spoke in that same strange speech. "Jeremiah, see if there's a critter or somethin' hidin' over there, where the fences come together." He was talking to the sentry coming back down the path, who sounded irritated.

"What's the matter, don't your legs work anymore?"

"Yeah, but I ain't got no shoes and there's a buncha cow poop down here. Just poke your rifle around where those fences come together, would ya?"

Rebekah pressed her body to the ground and opened her mouth to try to silence her breathing. She took short, silent breaths, trying not to move a muscle. The Confederate soldier was now directly behind her, swinging his rifle every few feet into the line of weeds in which she was hiding. She held her breath as he came closer, and when his rifle thrashed through the weeds right beside her, she prayed for mercy. The next sound she heard was his rifle hitting the fence post by her side. *Thank you, God!* she silently exclaimed as he continued past her to the end of the fence.

"There ain't nothin' here, Henry. Ya'll be seein' your fill of Yankees tomorrow, don't you fret."

They spoke for several more moments and then turned and walked in opposite directions. Thinking about their conversation, Rebekah realized that, although they had rifles and tried to sound tough, they were boys no older than her own sisters. What a waste the war was, she reflected; those two sentries, her "enemies," weren't much different from the boys she knew, the boys who would someday soon grow up and be husbands to girls like her and fathers to their children. Yet, one thing about them was different. If these barefoot Confederate boys won this war, slavery would continue. If they lost the war, slavery would end. The close call had almost paralyzed her, but this simple thought inspired Rebekah to regain her strength and nerve. She thought about her next move.

Chapter Seven
June 30, 1863, Night
Rebekah Sounds the Alarm

She knew this part of Marsh Creek very well. As it flowed downstream toward the east, the banks were soft and lined with trees. In the spring, the water filled the creek bed as wide as the border of trees, but now, in the hot, dry summer, what water there was flowed slowly in the middle, leaving the soft sides of the creek bed almost dry. She would be able to make good time walking beside the creek, out of sight behind the trees and bushes on the banks, with moonlight to guide her way. But first she had to get there. She resolved not to be careless again and set out on a slow crawl towards the creek, constantly keeping track of the positions of the sentries she knew of and on the lookout for others she had not yet seen. *Good thinking*, she commended herself, as she spotted a soldier walking on the far side of the creek. She took a moment to imagine how many families were being affected by this war in the same way as hers tonight. For a moment she wondered if perhaps there were other girls just like her, crawling through the fields and woods, trying to get to the Union army to warn them of the Confederate plan to move into Gettysburg. *Probably not*, she answered in her own mind, allowing herself to feel just a little proud.

When she made it to the creek bed, it was just as she had thought. The trees and bushes hid her from sight, and she was able to get to her feet and walk quickly. She constantly reminded herself to look up and around her, even though the natural thing was to look down to avoid stumbling. Every half-minute or so, she turned to look upstream from where she had come, aware now how quickly danger could present itself. She would soon be at the bridge where Marsh Creek flowed under Chambersburg Pike. She knew there would be soldiers guarding the bridge, based on what Lieutenant Barker had said yesterday. Rebekah felt her heart speed up even as her pace slowed as she rounded the bend where the bridge came into view.

Sure enough, almost a dozen figures were silhouetted against the starry sky on the west side of the bridge. As she checked their position and movements from behind a bush, she realized that their confidence in their numbers was making them less active and less alert than the single sentries she had passed by to get to Marsh Creek. Still, there were at least twenty eyes that could spot her if she tried to walk under the bridge. She felt the urge to just lie down and wait. She was exhausted. She was filthy.

No, I can't wait! Rebekah scolded herself. If she did not pass this bridge right now, it could be too late. The Confederates would get to Gettysburg first, grab the good ground, and win the war. Then Rebekah noticed that the soldiers were looking up the hill on the other side of the bridge. As she crept closer, she heard them discussing the number of Yankees that were looking down at them from the Gettysburg side. She reached down and grabbed some fresh mud to wipe onto her face, thinking her sweat had probably washed it clean. She could try to go around the bridge, but there were open fields on both sides. Suddenly her thoughts were interrupted by the sound of galloping horses. Not many, but enough to make all the men on the bridge grab their guns and look up the road toward Gettysburg. Before she had time to think better of it, she jumped to her feet and ran under the bridge.

She had never felt so light and fast in her life! The men on the bridge shouted for the horsemen to stop, and they did indeed slow down, but the sounds of their hoofs easily covered the quiet patter of her feet on the soft ground. She ran until she found a big bush to dive behind as the creek turned on the south side of the bridge. And only then did she realize what had happened. She had been on the other side of the bridge, racking her mind for a way to get past safely, when suddenly she was sprinting as fast as she could. *God is truly with me!* she exclaimed silently, sending up a prayer of thanks.

 She must make it to the Union Army. She could not be caught.

Her resolve had never been stronger as she crouched behind the bush, listening to the voices on the bridge. Their words were hard to understand, but there was no mention of General Stuart, so she could only assume that he was still somewhere out there, riding around in the night. She reminded herself to keep watching out for him as she slipped away from the bush and silently continued her trek in the soft bed of Marsh Creek.

For almost an hour, she continued to cover a lot of ground, staying alert just as she had on the north side of the bridge. Her pace slowed only a little as Marsh Creek turned south and the bed became very wide and very shallow. Because there was no bank to speak of, the farm fields came to the very edge of the creek and there were very few trees and bushes to hide her. But she hadn't seen any more soldiers and concluded that she had left behind the area where the Confederate Army was camping. Picking up her pace, she moved quickly through the water, stopping only occasionally for a cool drink.

Suddenly, a loud voice commanded, "Stop where you are!" Rebekah's heart skipped a beat as three men emerged from the shadows on the left side of the creek. She was overcome with disappointment. After all she had been through, she was caught anyway.

"Who are you?" One of them demanded.

As they came closer, she saw surprise in their faces. One, his eyes wide, looked down at her filthy but simple dress, devoid of the usual ruffles and buttons, and said in astonishment, "She's Amish!"

"She's what?" the one in front asked.

"It's a religious sect. They keep to themselves and have no part in this war. Very pious people. There are a lot of them back in Lancaster, where I'm from." Turning to the other man, he said, "I guess you don't see too many Amish up in Boston."

Rebekah felt a surge of relief. These men weren't Confederates; they were Yankees! She had made it to their lines after all.

"What are you doing here, young lady? It's almost midnight. And why are you all muddy? You git yourself lost, little girl?" the taller one asked.

After a moment of silence as Rebekah nervously looked at the faces of all three, she blurted: "I need to talk to your general. I need to talk to General Meade!"

They glanced at each other with amused smiles. With a chuckle, the one in front replied, "General Meade is miles from here, and he doesn't talk to little girls, especially, uh—what kind of religion are they?"

"Amish, she's Amish."

"Especially little Amish girls. Miss, you need to go home, wherever that is."

Looking down, she mumbled, "I can't." Then looking up at them, with as strong a voice as she could muster, "I can't!"

"Why not?"

"Because the Confederate officers are sleeping at our home, and they have it guarded. and I had to sneak out here to tell General Meade that they are planning on heading to Gettysburg in the morning."

All three of them looked at her incredulously, and then Rebekah added, "General Hill, the older one, was there this afternoon. He told the general that is staying at our house to lead them."

"You have a Confederate general staying at your house? Right now? Tonight?" replied the tall one, with a smile. "Which general, may I ask?"

"I think his name is Pettigrew, or something like that."

Looking first to the man on his right, then the one on his left, the man responded slowly, "That name is familiar, but I don't know who he is."

The man on the left shook his head to indicate he didn't know either, but the quiet one on the right finally spoke up. "I think he's from North Carolina. We ran into him on the Peninsula last year."

The tall one's face became serious, and he said, "We need to get her to Lieutenant Cunningham." He extended his hand to help her up the creek bed, but to his surprise she nimbly stepped up the bank by herself. Raising his eyebrows, he shrugged to the other two and walked with her to the horses they had been using to patrol the area. Grabbing the reins of their horses, they walked brickly with Rebekah to a small group of tents.

The taller went straight to the largest tent, bent down and pulled open the flap, calling softly: "Lieutenant Cunningham. … Sorry sir, but you need to wake up and see something." After hearing some grumbling from inside the tent, he stood back up and walked towards Rebekah and waited.

In a moment a young, vigorous-looking man came out of the tent, sleep still in his eyes, "This better be important, Corporal." Noticing Rebekah, he asked, "Who's she?"

"She's a girl that walked right into our picket line down by that creek. Private Johnson here says she's Amich."

"Amish! with an 'sh' on the end, like dish," corrected the shorter one.

"Why was she walking in the creek, at …"—he squinted to read the time on his pocket watch—"after eleven at night?" quite perturbed at being woken.

"Well, you see, Lieutenant, she says that there are a bunch of Confederate officers staying at her house, including a General Pettigrew."

Pondering this, while never taking his eyes off hers, he motioned to a log set beside a low-burning fire and said, "Sit her down there." With that he turned, reached into his tent, and pulled out a small stool. Settling down a few feet in front of Rebekah, he asked, "Where do you live, miss?"

"I live on a farm near Cashtown."

Without taking his wary eyes off her, he reached again into his tent, this time pulling out a rolled-up piece of parchment. He unrolled it and angled it so he could read it by the firelight. "Do you know the name of the road you live on?"

"The Chambersburg Pike." She was surprised at the strength of her voice. She didn't like it when people didn't take her seriously. She thought back to her conversation with Lieutenant Barker, the Confederate, the night before, and how she'd made it perfectly clear to him that she thought this war was about an unholy practice of slavery.

Rebekah thought of her mother. She wouldn't approve of Rebekah talking to these older men—these English men!—in such a bold and proud way. But she felt strong. She had never felt this way before.

"You live on the Chambersburg Pike, near Cashtown," Lieutenant Cunningham repeated, and paused as he held the map closer to the fire so he could read it. "Near to, uh, near to …"

"Gettysburg!" Rebekah blurted out. Turning her head and looking into the eyes of the ten or so Yankee soldiers who had now gathered around the fire to see this strange little girl, "and that's where they are going tomorrow! You need to get there first."

For a moment, nobody spoke. They looked around at each other, and then turned their eyes to Lieutenant Cunningham, who stared intently into Rebekah's eyes. "I'm taking her to Buford."

With that said, one of the younger men turned and quickly brought up a horse, handing the reins to Cunningham. He quickly mounted the horse and reached his hand down to Rebekah. "Get on up here, girl, you're coming with me." But Rebekah stayed seated on the log, saying nothing.

"Come on, I believe you, but we need to hurry!" Again, Rebekah sat and looked at him, not sure how to tell him how uncomfortable this suggestion made her. There was a long moment of silence as the men all stared at her.

Finally, Private Johnson took a step toward Cunningham and said quietly, "Lieutenant, she's an Amish girl. She's been taught not to mix with the outside world. She wouldn't ever get on the back of a horse with a strange man."

"She walked several miles through a Confederate picket line, for Pete's sake! I'm only taking her into Gettysburg so she can tell Buford what she just told us. And if she's right, we need to hurry!"

After a moment of thought, Private Johnson quietly suggested, "Perhaps we can hitch up a wagon, and sit her in the back?"

"Yeah, sure! But do it quickly! Let's go! Hitch up a couple of the bigger, faster horses, not those old broken-down nags, I want to get there before dawn."

In minutes, a wagon was ready, and Lieutenant Cunningham lowered the rear gate. Rebekah quickly jumped up from the log, ignored his proffered hand and leaped effortlessly into the back of the wagon. She slid across to sit on the opposite side of the wagon where Cunningham jumped up to sit.

"Okay, fine," the lieutenant said, resigned to doing whatever was needed to get this information to General Buford quickly. "Tie my horse to the rear of the wagon. And a couple of you men ride ahead and clear the pickets so I can get to Buford right away. I heard he's staying at a place called the Eagle Hotel."

With that, they were off on the fastest wagon ride Rebekah had ever been on. Her Daed never would have pushed the horses that fast. As they pulled into town, Cunningham pulled back on the reins and asked a sentry guarding the street, "Where's the Eagle Hotel?"

Apprehensive, but noting the gold bar on his shoulder straps, they pointed and said, "Down that road a few blocks."

As they pulled up to the front of the Eagle Hotel, the lieutenant seemed a bit nervous to Rebekah. On the trip to the hotel, Cunningham figured he would have to explain himself to a whole lot of officers before getting in front of Buford, and he planned on what he would say to them. Instead, General John Buford was sitting on the front porch talking to some officers. Cunningham saluted before climbing down from the wagon. He walked briskly around to the front of the horses just as a private reached out to grab the reins from him. By this time, Buford was halfway down the front steps of the hotel.

"General Buford, I am Lieutenant Cunningham of the —"

"I know who you are, Lieutenant. The question is, why are you racing this wagon into town? And why is there a little girl in the back? What is she, Amish?"

Knowing Buford was an impatient man—and seeing the other officers, including his immediate superior, Colonel Tom Devin, looking at him from the porch—he got to the point quickly. "General Buford, she says she lives on the Chambersburg Pike, part way from here to Cashtown. She said that there are a lot of Rebel officers staying at her house, including General Pettigrew. She says she overheard them saying they will all be coming to Gettysburg in the morning."

General Buford smoothed his mustache and walked slowly to the rear of the wagon so he could look into Rebekah's eyes. "When did they get there, miss?"

"Yesterday, 'round the afternoon. Four horsemen came up the side of Marsh Creek. Then a lot more came, and they are staying at our house, eating our food, and killing our chickens."

"What's the name of that creek that runs under the stone bridge on the Chambersburg Pike?" Buford asked no one in particular. The officers looked at each other, as a couple of them started pulling out maps. Lieutenant Cunningham spoke up. "It's Marsh Creek, sir." Nodding toward Rebekah, he added, "It's just as she said."

Looking back to Rebekah, Buford asked, "You mentioned General Pettigrew. Did you see any other officers?"

"There was a General Heth, but he was staying at the Cashtown Inn with a General Hill."

With that, General Buford's eyes opened wider. He glanced back at his officers on the porch. "That's A.P. Hill's Third Corps. If she's right, he's eight miles down that road right now!" He pointed west. "So Heth will be attacking early in the morning with his men, with the rest of the Third Corps and probably the rest of the Rebel army not far behind." Focusing again on Rebekah, he asked, "Did they discuss a General Stuart?"

"They said he must be riding around somewhere in the night, but I never saw him," she answered.

With that, Buford allowed himself a little chuckle, and with a nod to his staff, said, "We seem to know more about the location of the esteemed Rebel cavalry genius than his own superiors do!"

Turning to an aide at his side, he ordered, "Hitch two fresh horses to this wagon and tie two more to the back immediately! Lieutenant Cunningham, you drive back down that road to Emmitsburg as fast as these horses will take you and get in front of General Reynolds. Tell him what you know and deliver my letter to him." With that, several men unhitched the horses that had brought them to the Eagle Hotel, and other horses were quickly hitched up and the two spare horses were tied next to Lieutenant Cunningham's horse behind the wagon.

"Here you go." General Buford handed a short, scribbled note to Lieutenant Cunningham. Looking intently into his eyes, he said, "For God's sake, son, don't get lost!"

Nodding to Rebekah, Cunningham asked, "What about her?"

Rebekah started to feel afraid. Now that she had told them what she knew, what would they do with her?

"Take her with you," General Buford ordered. "If Reynolds doesn't believe you, have her tell him what she just told us."

The men quickly cleared from the street to get out of the way of the wagon as Cunningham wheeled it around. He tentatively glanced toward Colonel Devin, wondering if Devin would be proud of his actions or perturbed at him for going straight to Buford without conferring with him first. Colonel Devin gave an approving nod. Cunningham snapped the reins, and the wagon lurched forward.

As it disappeared around the corner, Buford turned to his officers. "Let's try to get a few hours' sleep, gentlemen. We will be in the fight of our lives tomorrow morning."

Colonel Devin stood tall and assured him, "I'll hold them off all day, General!"

Buford stopped and regarded him while pulling on his mustache. "No, you won't. They'll bring up more and more brigades until they force us back. But if we can hold them off long enough for General Reynolds to get here, and he can fight well when he gets here"—he turned and pointed south—"then we'll hold that ridge long enough for the rest of the army to get here. And on that high ground, we can win!

Now let's all grab some sleep. For some of us, it will be our last night on earth."

It took just over an hour for Lieutenant Cunningham to drive the wagon down Emmitsburg Pike. He stopped twice, once at his camp, to get four fresh men mounted up. They were told to ride ahead and alert the other pickets on Emmitsburg Pike that he was coming and was not to be stopped. His second stop was to quickly switch the horses after the first two tired. Rebekah had been on plenty of wagon rides in her life, but this midnight ride was by far the most terrifying experience she had ever endured.

Sensing her trepidation, he turned to her and assured her, "This is the road we rode up on. I remember it well."

But, considering how many times the wheels slipped off the edge of the road around the bends, she wasn't sure he remembered the road very well at all. At last, they slowed down. Looking up, she saw a dozen men ahead who had stopped Cunningham's riders and were waving at him to stop the wagon. Behind them, hundreds of fires glowed, revealing an encampment of thousands of tents.

"You're not going to see General Reynolds tonight, Lieutenant. Rest your horses and you can see him in the morning." The man was a lot older than the others and appeared to be in charge.

"Sergeant, I am not asking you. I am telling you. I have orders from General Buford to relay this message to General Reynolds immediately!" Cunningham hissed as he pulled out Buford's note. "We are the cavalry. Our job is to find the Rebs, and by God, we found them! They're going to attack Gettysburg in the morning, and General Reynolds needs to know that right now! So, take me to him, or there will be hell to pay for you in the morning."

The older man did not like being ordered about by Lieutenant Cunningham, who was at least fifteen years younger, but he was outranked, so he muttered to his men, "Take him to the staff headquarters."

In a few minutes, they pulled up to a group of much larger tents. A few smart-looking men were standing at a table, staring down at a large map by lantern light. Looking around, Rebekah noticed that most of the camp appeared to be asleep. Lieutenant Cunningham handed Buford's note to the men standing by the table and talked to them for a few moments, motioning toward Rebekah several times. Minutes later, one of the men left and Cunningham walked back to the rear of the wagon and lowered the gate. "Come on, get down. They want to talk to you."

By the time she had jumped down and walked to the table, the man who had left the table had returned with two men, a younger man and one who was dressed like General Buford. His ragged face and unkempt hair indicated to Rebekah that he had just woken from sleep. One of the men at the table turned to the younger man who had just arrived and said, "Lieutenant, you grew up in Chambersburg, correct?"

"Yes sir!" he said, eager to be of assistance to the higher-ranking men around him.

"Listen to what this little Amish girl tells General Wadsworth and let us know if this sounds correct, based upon what you know."

At that moment the older officer turned to Lieutenant Cunningham and said, "I'm General Wadsworth; you're First Cavalry Division, correct?" as he looked over Cunningham's uniform. "And this is the little Amish girl that's such a great spy?" he asked, not quite believing that he should have been woken so soon after retiring to his tent. "Tell me your story, miss."

Rebekah looked nervously around the table. Half of the men's faces were in the shadows, and all of them looked haggard. She'd never stayed up so late in her life, and she was suddenly exhausted. She felt like running back and lying down in the wagon. But she thought of Amos, Hannah, and Moses, and how everyone in both blue and gray uniforms had talked about getting to Gettysburg and getting "the good ground."

She felt her courage rise again. It was not an unfamiliar feeling, for she had grown up a strong girl, a girl who had always done what was needed at the moment. Calming an anxious animal or fighting off the Yoder brothers or even her own siblings—well, that she could do. But now, in the middle of the night, a half dozen grown English men, leaders of other men, were peering at her and evidently losing patience.

"Miss, we haven't got all night!" General Wadsworth said, without trying to hide his impatience. He was an older, very deliberate man, but after the long, hard marches of the past week, then being awakened from a much-needed sleep, he was in no mood to pamper her.

"General, I'll start," Lieutenant Cunningham said with a reassuring nod toward Rebekah. He handed General Wadsworth the short note from General Buford, then relayed how Rebekah had walked up the creek into his picket line a few hours ago. As he told the story, he stopped occasionally and asked Rebekah to fill in the details of the names of the road, the creek, and the officers she had seen. The whole time, the young officer from Chambersburg nodded affirmatively whenever one of the other officers looked at him to confirm the geography Rebekah described. When Lieutenant Cunningham finished, there was a moment of silence. Rebekah understood that they were digesting what they had just heard, but they all just stood there looking at her, before slowly turning their heads toward General Wadsworth.

"Did they discuss a General Stuart, a cavalry commander?" Wadsworth asked.

"They complained that he was somewhere riding around in the night, but they had not heard from him."

Wadsworth paused; then, looking around at each of his staff, he said, "Then they don't know where we are, how close we are." He paused again, deep in thought, his eyes staring down at the map on the table. Finally, he declared, "Very well, this makes sense. General Lee wants to consolidate all his divisions in Gettysburg, pick the high ground, and wait for us. But we'll get moving now. I don't want to wake up General Reynolds just yet. If all this plays out, we'll need him to be fresh in the morning to lay out the battle. And I know this is what he would do, anyway. When he awakes, I'll tell him what we did."

"General, are you sure about this? What if General Reynolds wants to check with General Meade before he moves any troops? How do you know if any of this is true?"

"General Meredith, I will take responsibility for this. If this girl is correct, and Buford believes she is—and I am inclined to believe her as well—then we must get to Gettysburg before the Rebels can get there." Holding up the note from Buford, General Wadsworth said, "Buford has identified a high ridge just south of town. For once, we'll hold the good ground! But only if we move quickly."

Turning to the two men who were at the table when Cunningham pulled up with Rebekah, he said: "You've been laying out the order of march, correct?"

"Yes sir, we'll leave at dawn."

"No, we won't. That will be too late. Wake the men now. We'll leave as soon as we can and put the Iron Brigade up front. When the Rebs come down that Chambersburg Pike in the morning, they will know the battle is on when they see the Black Hats! Let's move, gentlemen, let's move!"

Before the general could walk away, Lieutenant Cunningham asked, "May I leave now sir? I want to be leading my men in the morning when this fight gets started."

General Wadsworth nodded and with a slight smile said, "Yes lieutenant, you get back up there, and you hold them off until we can get there. And for God's sake, Lieutenant, hold that good ground!"

"What about her?" Cunningham asked, nodding to Rebekah. He was hoping Wadsworth would not tell him to take her back with him, because he wanted to get on his horse and ride as quickly as he could back to his men. Glancing around, he was overwhelmed by how bizarre the scene was. All these officers, standing in a pool of lantern light in the middle of the night, planning a battle for tens of thousands of men—and all because of what this little Amish girl standing beside him told them.

General Wadsworth turned to one of the younger men at the table and said, "Take her and the wagon down to where the 11th Corps medical camp is; they'll take care of her."

In an instant, everyone was in motion. Officers went to rouse others from their tents so they could wake their men and get them moving, marching towards Gettysburg, knowing what that would mean for them.

The young officer tasked with taking Rebekah to the medical corps encampment seemed none too happy with his orders. "Let's go!" he grumbled. As he grabbed the reins of the wagon, Rebekah jumped into the back. Lieutenant Cunningham untied his horse from the back of the wagon and mounted it for the ride back to his camp and his men. The four men who had ridden ahead of the wagon on the way down from Gettysburg were already mounted and eager to leave. Cuningham turned his horse around, but just before galloping off, he looked down at Rebekah. He paused for a moment and said, "Thank you." With that, he spurred his horse forward.

"Lieutenant!" Rebekah heard herself yell in a voice louder than she thought she could make and paused as Cunningham pulled back on the reins and turned his horse sideways so he could face her. "Don't get killed." He nodded, and then galloped off into the darkness. She wondered if she would ever see him again. She said a prayer for his safety.

The wagon moved off in the opposite direction. The trip took just long enough for Rebekah to fall asleep. When the wagon stopped, she heard the driver say something to a soldier standing in front of them, who then waved them past. A short time later, the wagon stopped in front of a group of tents and Rebekah heard the officer having a brief discussion with someone, which Rebekah could not understand. The driver seemed to become more irritated as they waited. After a few minutes, a woman came to the back of the wagon, lowered the gate and smiled at Rebekah, and kindly invited Rebekah to follow her. As soon as she got off the back of the wagon, the officer in the driver's seat immediately snapped the reins and the wagon turned back in the direction they had come from. The woman said nothing, but led Rebekah to a large tent and motioned her to go inside. Stepping over some sleeping people, she laid down a blanket for Rebekah and whispered, "Good night." Rebekah immediately fell asleep.

Chapter Eight
July 1, 1863, Morning
Doctor Hovey and His Family

"Miss, wake up, we're pulling out." Seeing the low sunshine flooding in through the tent opening, Rebekah knew it was early morning. The woman who had woken her closed the tent flap and looking around, she realized she was alone. Whoever had been sleeping in the tent when she came in were gone, their blankets gone as well. Rebekah stood, folded the blanket, and slipped out into the sunshine, her mind jostled by the intense noise and energy of an army breaking camp. Glancing around the rolling hills, she saw the last of the tents being taken down, wagons being loaded, horses being tied to the wagons and, in the distance, men on the march, thousands of them. They were coming from various directions, but they all ended up on the main road, heading to Gettysburg. She thought of Lieutenant Cunningham, the General Buford that she met last night, the Confederate Lieutenant Barker and his General Pettigrew. She realized that they would all be part of the battle that was about to take place. Perhaps it had already started. But she didn't have time to think about it.

"Hey, just don't stand there. Give me a hand with the tent!"

She looked around and saw a boy about her age taking down the tent she had slept in. She walked to the opposite side and copied what he was doing, pulling down ropes and posts, and then pulling out the stakes.

"My name is Frank; I'm an orderly working for my father," he said, nodding towards the man who was loading a covered wagon. He was handing the blankets and boxes to a woman inside the wagon, who was stacking them neatly.

"Remember to leave space for the little girl," the man said.

Frank pointed to one side of the tent and said, "Help me roll it tight, so it won't take up a lot of space. We're loaded full up with supplies. We're all expecting a big battle soon."

As they loaded the tent and then the rest of the cooking wares into the wagon, two other wagons pulled up, apparently waiting for them to get going.

"Hi Miss, I'm Marilla Hovey," the woman said as she stepped down from the wagon. "That is my husband, Dr. Hovey. He's a surgeon for the Eleventh Corps, and you met my son Frank. What's your name, honey?"

"Rebekah."

"That's a fine Christian name. I understand you are Amish?" Rebekah nodded, realizing that she was no longer wearing her bonnet. She could not remember where and when she had lost it, but she knew that without it on her head she would not stand out as Amish quite as readily.

"My, you sure are filthy!" Mrs. Hovey did not mean it to be an insult, and Rebekah did not take it as such. Mrs. Hovey was right, she was filthy. She had torn her dress jumping down from the porch, rolled on dead chicken heads, lain in dust and mud, then deliberately rubbed it all over her and then splashed through a creek.

"We'll be setting off as soon as Bleeker finishes up with the other surgeons; he likes to talk," Mrs. Hovey said with a slight smile.

Rebekah noticed that Dr. Hovey was talking to a man on a horse, who had ridden up to where the two wagons were waiting. Rebekah remembered him as one of the men standing around the table when Lieutenant Cunningham brought her to the headquarters last night. He was motioning with his hands in the direction of the road where the troops and wagons were all moving on. He pointed behind him, and

Rebekah heard him say "Gettysburg." As he finished, he nodded to Rebekah and, with a smile on his face, spoke to the men longer. When he was done, he saluted, turned his horse around, and galloped to the road.

Dr. Hovey came back and said, "We will leave as soon as we get the wagon hitched up. Frank, give me a hand with the horses. Get the three old nags, I'll get the big guy." Rebekah watched as Frank hitched up the three older horses. He did all right with them at first, but then he got them turned the wrong way and could not get them hitched. She felt like helping but decided that they must do this a lot, so she just watched. Dr. Hovey had a bit of trouble with the big stallion, and again, Rebekah refrained from helping. At last, the horses were properly hitched to the wagon and they were ready to go.

"The Army gives me three old nags and a horse that isn't even broken! Well, let's go!" he said, jumping onto the driver's seat. Frank jumped up next and sat on a box inside the wagon behind Dr. Hovey. Mrs. Hovey nodded for Rebekah to jump up and sit beside him, but Rebekah did not move. She looked at Rebekah for a moment and then said, "Oh, I understand. Frank, jump in the front seat with your Pa and I'll ride in the back with Rebekah." She gave Rebekah a knowing smile, realizing that an Amish girl would consider it improper to sit in the back of a wagon with a boy, especially an English boy.

When the three wagons carrying the surgeons rolled up to the road, a man on horseback rode up and stopped them. A long line of men marched ten across. In many ways they looked just like the Confederate troops that had been lined up in front of her house the morning before. They had that same kind of gun, blanket roll, canteen, and the same determined look, but these men wore blue uniforms, and they all had shoes.

When that marching column passed, and before the next column approached, the officer signaled for the surgeon's wagons to move forward. The horses pulled on command, following the troops ahead.

As Rebekah settled herself into a gap between two boxes, the woman smiled at her and said, "You must be hungry. Here, I saved this from our breakfast." She handed Rebekah a loosely wrapped cloth with some corn bread and blackberries inside. The blackberries instantly reminded Rebekah of home. Could it really be less than two days ago that she was picking blackberries when Lieutenant Barker and the other Confederate horsemen rode down Marsh Creek? Oh, how she longed for home! While she felt safe riding in the wagon with Dr. Hovey and his family, she knew she was a long way from her home. And, because she had snuck out in the night, her family did not know where she was. Plus, thousands of blue-clad soldiers as well as Confederates were marching between her and them. "I hope it's worth it," she said softly under her breath.

"What's that, miss?" Mrs. Hovey asked. Rebekah had said it louder than she thought.

"I hope all these men can get to Gettysburg in time to get the good ground they all talk about. I just want this war to be over and the slaves to be free."

"We all do, honey, we all do. Now, go to sleep. If this battle is as big as they're all saying it will be, we will have plenty of wounded men to take care of. You can stay with us until the battle is over, and then we'll get you back to your home as soon as we can."

Mrs. Hovey paused, reached out her hand to rest it on Rebekah's knee and then, with a voice full of admiration, said, "You did a very brave thing, Rebekah. I don't understand all the movements of the army, or even how you got here, but they are all saying your information led these troops to get moving quickly, and now we hear that there is already fighting at Gettysburg."

Dr. Hovey, with his hands on the reins, turned and added, "From what I heard this morning, you caused quite a stir at First Corps headquarters this morning. General Reynolds was woken at 4 a.m. when his staff received a note from General Meade telling him to get moving toward Gettysburg. When he found out that General Wadsworth had already put the First Division on the road, he was furious. But when Wadsworth told him about you and showed him Buford's letter, he realized Wadsworth did the right thing. He is probably almost to Gettysburg now." Even their son, Frank, turned and gave her a respectful smile.

Rebekah tried to sleep. She was exhausted. But she thought about what Mrs. Hovey had said about having to take care of wounded soldiers. She was good with animals and tended to them when they were hurt. She had also helped her Mamm when one of the boys got cut up. But she couldn't help feeling uneasy when she thought about tending to wounded men. Her fear got worse as they got closer to Gettysburg. As they approached the town, she thought she heard thunder, and bent forward so she could look around the top of the wagon and see clouds. She saw none.

Leaning back, she noticed a different look on Mrs. Hovey's face. "It's not thunder, honey, it's cannon fire. They're already fighting. So, when we get there, we will need to get set up in a hurry and get ready for the wounded."

Mrs. Hovey's motherly demeanor was gone, and her voice was full of trepidation. Rebekah suddenly felt a tinge of tension in her stomach. She looked out the side of the wagon, which was headed vaguely in the direction of her home.

She realized she had never thought of a plan to get back home when she crept out of her house and walked down Marsh Creek last night. And now, she thought with some shame, her family would be sick with worry about her, not knowing where she had disappeared to. As the wagon drove up the road Lieutenant Cunningham had raced down last night, her thoughts vacillated between thinking of Amos, Hannah, and Moses, to what it would be like when the wagon stopped and they started to treat wounded men. Tears came to her eyes as she thought about her mother. She loved her sisters and brothers, and certainly her Daed. But there was a special place in her heart for her mother. She dozed for a few moments but was awakened by louder cannon fire.

Dr. Hovey turned and said, "They're bringing up reinforcements. More men and more cannon. It's going to be a big one." The smile he'd had for Rebekah when they left camp was gone. His forehead became furrowed, his lips pressed tightly together.

"When we get there, Rebekah, just stay close to me," Mrs. Hovey said as she reached out her hand again and set it on the girl's knee. Rebekah forced a smile, grateful for the reassuring gesture from this English lady.

"Are all mothers like that?" she wondered. It was like Mrs. Hovey was reading her mind and could sense all her fears.

No one spoke the last few miles toward the outer edge of the battle. Twice their wagon and the others from the medical corps were ordered to pull off the road, as more men and ammunition wagons joined the race toward Gettysburg. As the pounding of the cannon fire grew louder, they were instructed to turn right on a smaller road and then go north again toward Gettysburg. Mrs. Hovey reached into the back of the wagon and pulled out a basket that held more cornbread, some beef jerky, and berries.

"Eat up. We'll be too busy when we get there!" she said as she passed the basket around.

As they approached Gettysburg, they were stopped at an intersection by a mounted Yankee, apparently a man the Hovey's knew.

"Good afternoon, Doctor, it's good to see you. From what I hear, you will be quite busy!" Turning in his saddle, he pointed north, toward the fighting. "You're on the Taneytown Road. Up ahead, there's a little road to your right, not much wider than a farm road. Granite Schoolhouse Road. You can see a small schoolhouse on the north side of it. Make a right there, and just before you get over to the next big road, the Baltimore Pike, the 11th Corps hospital is being set up." Doctor Hovey repeated the directions to make sure he understood them, then snapped the reins smartly, urging the horses to pick up the pace.

It was mid-afternoon when they arrived at the farm being set up as the camp for the 11th Corps hospital. It was a big farm, with a very large barn and a nice home beyond it. It reminded Rebekah of her family's farm, including the built-up mound of earth on the front side of the barn to allow wagons and animals to walk into the top floor. The bottom floor opened to the back. Like the barn on their farm, the upper level that extended about a man's height past the rear wall of the lower level, creating a forebay.

"Over here, Dr. Hovey!" a man said, waving as he hurried toward the wagon. "We're getting the surgeon tables set up under the forebay. If your kids could get the animals out of the barn and clear out the hayloft, that would be helpful!" With that, he hurried on to give the same instructions to wagons that followed. Rebekah noted no one corrected the man to say that she was not, like Frank, one of the Hovey children. But it didn't matter. They were instantly too busy.

Dr. and Mrs. Hovey unpacked their medical supplies in the forebay and set up a makeshift table, using one of the rear doors of the barn. Frank said he was going up to help remove the hay from the top of the barn. Rebekah instinctively grabbed the reins of the horses attached to the Hovey wagon, unhitched them and led the team down to a lower fenced field. Keeping the horses tied together loosely, she tied them to a pasture fence at a spot where they could graze a little and drink from a small creek that ran through the property.

Looking around, it shocked her to see the farm disintegrating even faster than when the Confederates arrived at her family's place. Wooden fences were taken down to be used for firewood, and troops, wagons and then cannon kept arriving, trampling down the tender fields of crops and hay. As she walked back up to the barn, Mrs. Hovey met her and grabbed her hand.

"Come with me," she said, leading her away from the barn and toward the house. "This is Mrs. Spangler," she said, introducing the woman who was standing near the back door. "This is her house, her farm. Her family has stayed and they want to help. When the wounded come, we'll need water, lots of it. There's a well in front of the summer kitchen right here, and there are several creeks on the farm. I will be down at the barn with Dr. Hovey and Frank, helping with the surgeries." She looked at the barn, and then turned back to Rebekah and said with a furrowed brow, "Try to stay away from the barn, all right?" Rebekah nodded, although she wondered why Mrs. Hovey wanted to keep her away.

Mrs. Spangler interrupted her thoughts. "Come with me. We're rolling bandages, and from the sound of all those guns, we will need a lot of them." Rebekah followed her into the summer kitchen, a separate building beside the main house that was large enough for a table. A large fireplace and bread oven took up wall at the far end. Rebekah noted the main house was made of stone, like her own. A young soldier not much older than Rebekah was showing two girls about her sisters' age how to tear sheets into strips and then roll the strips to serve as bandages.

Mrs. Spangler introduced them. "These are my daughters, Harriet and Sabina." Rebekah could see that they were farm girls, good with their hands, but they looked scared. As Rebekah sat down, she realized she probably looked scared as well. She *was* scared.

Not much later, the first wagonload of wounded men arrived, driving down the Baltimore Pike from Gettysburg. There were several other wagons right behind the first. Rebekah had never seen wagons like this. She heard the others refer to them as ambulances. They were smaller than the typical farm wagon Rebekah was used to and carried a team of three men each. On the first wagon, five soldiers were sitting in the back on benches, all of them wrapped in bandages soaked red with blood. Some had more than one wound. Some of the following wagons had three men lying in the back, each laid out on a cloth bed supported by poles on each side. The ambulance crews referred to them as stretchers. When the wagon stopped in front of the barn, the men in the wagons unloaded them. The worst cases were led or carried to the forebay at the back of the barn, where the Hovey's and other medical teams were waiting. Others were being treated and sent up around the front of the barn and laid inside to rest.

As more and more wounded arrived, they were helped off the wagons and placed in the fields around the barn. Mrs. Spangler gave Rebekah a bucket and a metal cup. "Give each of the wounded a drink and get to as many of them as you can!"

Rebekah, observing Mrs. Spangler's pale face, thought she must be feeling sick seeing the horrid scenes unfolding on her farm, which just a few hours earlier had been one of the best-kept properties around. As the afternoon gave way to evening, the flow of wounded just kept coming. Rebekah went from man to man, giving each a drink, trying to do her part to comfort them, while fighting off nausea. The stench of the bleeding, sweating men overwhelmed her, plus many of them had lost control of their bowels.

But it was the cries of the wounded men that really devastated her. A couple of times, she saw that one was lying motionless—dead!—still waiting to be seen by the doctors. She walked away from those men quickly. She dared not go near the forebay in the rear of the barn where the surgeries were taking place and agonizing screams could be heard every few minutes.

Overwhelmed, and with her bucket empty, she returned to the well by the kitchen, but it had been pumped so many times already it seemed to be running dry. Her efforts brought only a trickle of water. She remembered the teaching at last Sunday's meeting, about how Jesus said, "I was thirsty, and you gave me drink." That was how Christians show their love for God, the teacher said, by treating everyone like they were Jesus, simply caring for them in their time of need. But now even that was becoming impossible!

Overwhelmed by despair, she felt her legs wobble. She sat down on the bucket and started to cry. Her head in her hands, she repeated over and over, "I can't do this, I can't do this!"

After a few minutes, she felt a hand come to rest on her shoulder. Looking up through teary eyes, she saw Mrs. Hovey looking down at her. Her dress was stained with blood, but her reassuring eyes comforted Rebekah. "Honey, I know this is awful for you, but I have noticed you and you are doing great work. Water is not only a comfort to these men, but also helping them stay alive. Without it they may die. The bleeding makes them lose water, so they need you." Mrs. Hovey gently brushed the sweaty hair off Rebekah's teary face. "When one of the boys from the town Dr. Hovey and I came from was brought to the cutting table, he recognized us and told us to thank you for the drink. You should know that."

Rebekah looked up at her through her tears. For a moment, amidst all the horrid turmoil, their eyes connected, and they shared their grief. "Did he, the boy from your town, make it?"

Mrs. Hovey herself now teared up and, unable to swallow, just shook her head. Mrs. Hovey had worked with her husband in his practice in upstate New York for years, and they had doctored the poor soldier from the time he was born. Instinctively, Rebekah stood up and hugged her. For a moment, they shared their grief and gained strength from each other. But then, grasping Rebekah's shoulders, Mrs. Hovey said fiercely, "But there are others. Hundreds! We must help them."

"But the well is going dry—there is no more water."

Mrs. Hovey had regained her strength and composure. "Then go to the creek down there. There must be water, and these men need it. I know you can do this, Rebekah!" As she turned to head back to the barn, she looked around and gave Rebekah the briefest smiles, which made Rebekah feel strong again.

"I will do it. I can do it!" she said out loud to herself as she reached for the bucket. She went to the small creek where she had tied up the horses. But now there were now scores of horses in the field and the creek had become muddy and foul. Running upstream, she found another spot where the water was still clean. *This will do*, she thought, dipping the bucket into the deepest pool she could find. With renewed strength, she hurried to where the men were being taken off the ambulances. She was startled to find that some of the wounded men now were wearing gray—Confederates! She wondered if some of them had slept at her farm last night, but there was no time for talking.

Another ambulance came in, full of men sitting on the benches on both sides of the wagon. She hurried to the back of the wagon when it stopped and, dipping the cup into the bucket, gave each man a full cup as they were eased down to the ground by the wagon crew. Focusing on giving each man a full cup without spilling any, she paid no attention to their faces. The last man off the wagon, taking the cup gratefully, said, "Thank you, Rebekah." It was Lieutenant Cunningham! Dried blood crusted the left side of his face, and a blood-soaked bandage had been tied around his head. His left arm and hand were also wrapped with another bloody bandage.

Gasping, she blurted out, "Oh no, not you too? How bad is it?"

"The head wound looks a lot worse than it is, I think. But I believe they will have to amputate at least part of my hand."

"What happened?" she asked, but before he could answer, she realized the answer was obvious. "Where did it happen?"

Nodding his head toward Gettysburg, he said, "Right over there, on the Western edge of town. We rode hard last night when we left you. When I got back, my men were already awake and breaking camp. We rode through Gettysburg and lined up just west of town across Chambersburg Pike. It was shortly after dawn—and you were right, General Heth and his men came at us. But we fought a lot harder than they expected cavalry to fight. They backed off until they could bring up the rest of their division, and then they came at us again. But as we were faltering, the Iron Brigade came up the Emmitsburg Pike, from where we were last night."

He paused, looked at her and said, "Because of you, they got there in time, just in time. If they had been any later, the day would have been lost. As it was, in the afternoon more and more Rebs came up Chambersburg Pike, and then a lot of others attacked from the north of town. They hit us real hard, and we retreated through the town. It was all confusing, but General Buford re-formed us up in lines on top of the slopes south of town on that ridge right over there."

As he talked, he pointed toward the higher ground just beyond the farm. "That's where I was hit by canister from cannon fire. But we delayed the Rebs just long enough for more of our troops to arrive and form up on top of the ridge, and now we have the high ground."

Pausing, he looked at her, and noticed the blood, sweat and tears, caked with dust, all over her face, arms and dress. "You did real well, Rebekah, real well." With that he turned and walked toward the barn. Rebekah stood and watched him, relieved that he was at least on his feet. She turned, picked up her empty pail and hurried down to the creek to refill it.

As the pace of the arriving ambulances picked up, Rebekah noticed that one ambulance crew looked different from the others. Other than Elijah, the men on the wagon were the first black men she had seen up close. As they unloaded the wounded soldiers in the back, they could not help but notice Rebekah staring at them. The thought occurred to her that while this war was being fought over slavery, these were the first black men she had seen in the Army. None of the wounded men were black. After giving a drink to each of the wounded men, she passed her cup to the ambulance driver. When he was finished, she dipped it again and handed it to another ambulance man. "Are there other black men in the Army?" she asked the driver.

"Yes," he replied, "but not as soldiers with guns."

"But that's a-changin'," his friend commented. "There's entire Negro units trainin' right now, up in Massachusetts and elsewhere."

"We want to fight as soldiers, and not just to free our brethren," the driver continued. After a moment's thought, he turned his back to Rebekah and lifted his shirt. She was startled to see horrific scars across his back. He said, "I'm lookin' to find the man who gave me these whippin's. He gave some to my mama too, and I'll be lookin' to pay him back."

"Well, why wouldn't the Army let you fight, if the war is about slavery?" Rebekah asked.

"Miss," the driver explained, "most of the men in this army want the slaves to be freed, but they don't want us to be their equals. That's why they didn't allow us to be real soldiers."

"But now, after so many white men have been killed, they need us, so they're gonna give us guns too," his friend added.

Rebekah just stood, looking back and forth at the three of them. They looked like men to her, no different really than white men. But she remembered that she had known Elijah for years because her Daed did business with Mr. Mickley. But her Mamm and older sisters had probably never spoken to a black man, and neither did many others in Cashtown, especially the Amish. It occurred to her that neither her Daed nor Mr. Mickley had ever said anything about Elijah being black.

They just treated him as a man. She remembered the story in the Bible of the Samaritan woman at the well. If Jesus could look past the facts that she was a woman, a Samaritan, and an adulterer and offer her eternal life, then she should certainly treat others with that same spirit.

"Miss, we thank you for the drink, but we gotta get back to the fightin'. There are men that need us right now."

With that they climbed back onto the wagon and turned back onto Baltimore Pike, heading toward the sounds of battle north of town. As Rebekah walked back to the creek to fill her bucket, she thought about their conversation and realized she didn't even know the men's names. "Well," she thought, "the driver had scars from being whipped, so I will just call him Amos, after the man in the pamphlet the abolitionist gave me." She thought about that day, which now seemed so long ago, and that made her think of her father and how much she missed him.

It had been a hot day, and it was still hot as the sun set. Rebekah's legs ached with fatigue. For hours, she had been scurrying up and down the rolling hills of the Spangler farm, lugging the heavy water pail. But she was a strong farm girl, used to hard work. Long after sunset, the ambulances continued to bring the wounded in, and Rebekah continued to bring water to them. Finally, long after the bright moon rose, the exhaustion of the previous night and the long, horrid day caught up with her. She found her way back to the wagon she had ridden in on, slipped behind the seat, and instantly fell into a sound sleep.

Chapter Nine
July 2, 1863
Rebekah Takes the Lead

Cannon fire woke Rebekah shortly after dawn as the battle entered a second day. She momentarily forgot where she was and how she got there. But when she sat up, it all came back to her in a moment. The wagon, the stench, and the collective moans and cries of hundreds of wounded men brought the reality of her situation back to her immediately.

She felt a strong pang of hunger and remembered she hadn't eaten a thing since her small lunch the day before in the wagon. Walking toward the house, she noticed smoke pouring out of the chimneys of both the house and the summer kitchen. She found Frank Hovey tending to the fires, noticing that he was feeding cut-up fence posts into the flames. Mrs. Spangler was there, too, baking bread as fast as she could. She smiled and broke a piece of fresh bread off a warm loaf and handed it to Rebekah. "Eat up, child, you will need your energy. My son, Beniah, is going to help you as well." She nodded to a boy sitting at the table. He looked up at her in between bites, his bloodshot eyes showing the effects of the exhaustion and terror that yesterday had brought. He seemed to be about her age. She had not seen him yesterday, but he must have been busy helping in some way.

She realized that, in addition to all the suffering he was experiencing, he was also witnessing the destruction of his farm.

Rebekah had been raised to respect boys, and she fully expected to respect and honor her husband when she grew up, as Mamm did Daed. But she also realized that she might just have more internal strength than this boy did, just as she had more strength than her younger brothers.

Sitting down across from him, she gave him a reassuring smile and said, "I'll show you; we'll do it together." After finishing their quick breakfast, they stood up to face the day. "You will need a bucket and a cup." When he returned, she led him to the creek where she had been getting water late last night. But there were more horses there now, dropping manure and stomping around, muddying the waters. The water at that spot was fouled too. "Is there another creek around here?" she asked Beniah.

"Down there, beyond the orchard," he said, pointing toward the lower part of the farm.

"Let's go; you lead the way." She didn't want to sound bossy, but she needed to convince him that there was a lot of work to be done, and they needed to get to it. The ambulances were already arriving with more wounded men, though not as many as the night before. With two of them working together, they quickly caught up with giving water to the soldiers as they arrived and then the men who had been wounded the previous day and were convalescing in the top level of the barn or lying in the fields beyond.

Walking up the ramp to the upper level of the barn, she was shocked to see it completely full. These men had been treated, so they were somewhat clean and had fresh bandages. As she stepped through the rows of men to give them water, she was horrified to see how many were missing a leg, a hand, or an arm. She thought that just that morning these men had been so young and healthy, and now they were crippled for life.

"This is why we strive to live in peace with all men, so far as it is up to us," Rebekah remembered her father saying. "We do not kill, nor do we make war. The godly do not involve themselves in worldly conflicts. As the scripture says, "Do not resist the evil doer who slaps you but turn to him the other cheek. If thine enemy hunger, feed him; if he thirsts, give him drink. Be not overcome with evil but overcome evil with good.'"

But she could not bear to dwell on it now. She had to get them water. Turning toward the door, she said, "Beniah, let's go refill our buckets." He looked pale and seemed unable to move at the horror of it all, so she gently grabbed him by the arm and led him out of the barn. "Look, I don't want to be here either. But just think about what we must do. We can't change any of this, we can only relieve their suffering, and most importantly, help them live!"

In the afternoon a large column of troops arrived, marching up the Baltimore Pike from the south. They looked exhausted, but the soldiers already on the farm began to cheer as they came into view. Rebekah didn't understand all they said, but did hear one exulting, "Uncle John Sedgewick and the 6th Corps are here! We'll give the Rebs hell now!" As soon as the columns of weary troops stopped, they pulled off the road and headed to the same creek as Beniah and Rebekah were getting their water from. Horses and men jumped in the water to cool off and to quench their thirst.

"Beniah, is there another creek on your property?"

He looked around and said, "No, that's it."

"Well, is there a large creek nearby?"

He pointed down the road. "There's Rock Creek."

"How far away?" Rebekah gazed down the road.

"See that stone bridge? That's the bridge for the Baltimore Pike over Rock Creek."

Rebekah realized the distance was far too great to carry buckets back and forth from. "Okay, we will need to get a wagon and a lot of buckets. You gather buckets, tubs, anything that will hold water. I'll hitch up the horses to the wagon we rode in on."

Rebekah made her way to where she had tied up the Hovey's team of horses the day before. The entire pasture was filled with horses, but she found the Hovey's team. The commotion of the newly arriving men and horses and the cries of the wounded had put the horses on edge, especially the young stallion. Rebekah untied the three old nags first, swinging them easily in front of the Hovey wagon and hitching them up. The stallion was another matter, so she just patted his nose and whispered to him for a while. "Come on, big guy, it will be fine." He wasn't as big or temperamental as her Thunder, but he certainly was a big, strong horse. After some gentle coaxing, she was able to get him hitched to the wagon alongside the other horses.

Rebekah and Beniah then loaded up the wagon with all the pails and two large drums he had rolled down from the side of the barn. Then they paused for a moment, each waiting for the other to assume the driver's seat. Rebekah was good at handling horses, but steering a wagon was another matter altogether. Daed had always done that.

Finally, Rebekah asked Beniah, "Do you know how to steer a wagon?"

"Sure," he replied, hesitantly because he'd become accustomed to following Rebekah's lead. She always seemed to know what to do next. "I've steered wagons all around our farm, and Pa has let me drive into Gettysburg a few times."

"Then jump up," Rebekah said as she walked around the horses and climbed up onto the passenger's seat. Beniah turned the wagon around and steered it onto their farm road toward Baltimore Pike. He held the reins tight, carefully and skillfully steering the team around ambulances and wounded men. When they got to the Pike, he turned right heading south, away from Gettysburg. New troops were still arriving from that direction, so Beniah had to steer around them, often onto the side of the road. He looked a bit nervous, so Rebekah gave him her most reassuring smile and said, "You're doing well."

The bridge wasn't that far by wagon, and just before they got to it, Beniah pulled off to the left side, off the road. That was the upstream side of Rock Creek, so the water was clean even though the troops and horses had fouled it on the Spangler farm side of the road as it flowed downstream. He turned the wagon around beside a tree, and Rebekah jumped down to tie the horses to a low branch. She was extra careful to secure the stallion. Then they took the smaller buckets two at a time down to the creek. They filled them with clean, fresh water and walked them to the back of the wagon, where the two big barrels were.

"I'll jump up," Beniah offered. Rebekah noted growing confidence in his voice. She handed the buckets to him one at a time, but they were heavy, and her shoulders ached after the second trip back from the creek. She remembered that when she and her brothers had been helping their father build the side porch, she couldn't lift the shingles up to him, but her brothers could. Dejected, she had walked over to Mamm, who pointed out, "Girls have strong legs, but boys have strength in their arms and shoulders so they can pick things up above their heads better."

"Beniah, I'll jump up this time." Switching places helped, as Beniah had no trouble lifting the buckets up to Rebekah, who only had to lift them to about waist level before dumping them in the barrels. After a few more trips, the barrels were full, and they untied the horses and climbed back in the wagon.

"Let's go!" Beniah urged with a gentle snap on the reins, but the horses struggled to move the heavy wagon. The nags, Rebekah could understand, but the stallion should have been strong enough to pull harder. The boy snapped the reins again and yelled, "Let's go!" louder. But still no movement.

"Hold on a moment," Rebekah said as she jumped down. When she landed, she realized that the ground was soft, and she noticed the wagon wheels were sinking under the heavy load of the water. She thought about emptying some of the water out of the barrels to lighten it, but remembering all the wounded men still arriving, she instead walked up to the stallion and said firmly, "Listen, you are going to lead this team back to the road." Her voice was stronger this time, and she certainly meant it.

She grabbed his harness and directed Beniah, "Snap the reins!" As he did, she gave the harness a strong pull, looked the stallion in the eye and commanded him: "Move!" And he did! Rebekah could not help but marvel at how strong the horse really was, and she led him back onto the road, where the surface was hard and firm. Pausing, she smiled and praised him: "Good boy, good boy." Realizing that some troops on the road had stopped to watch them, she climbed back into the wagon and told Beniah to head back up the road towards the farm.

A horseman rode up beside the wagon and, in a surprised tone, asked, "Where did you learn to talk to horses, young girl?"

"On my father's farm," she replied, without taking her eyes off the road.

"You're Amish, ain't ya?" he asked, looking up and down at her torn and soiled dress. "But where's your hat?"

She thought about ignoring him, but he didn't seem eager to leave.

"I lost it. We've been busy with the wounded."

"Well, I just want to tell you that you handled those horses real well," he said, pausing, and with a bit of a snicker, "for a little Amish girl."

"Thanks." It was a curt reply, meant to end the conversation, and it did. The horseman turned and rode back down the road to his men. As they approached the road to the Spangler farm, Beniah first turned the wagon back onto the little road that led to the barn. But then he steered it off the road to the right, toward the top of the rising pasture.

"It will be easier for us to carry the water downhill than up. I'll hold the reins. Jump down and tie the horses up by that stone wall," he said.

That turned out to be a fine idea. With the water in the barrels so close by, they were able to get it to the wounded quicker than before. They made two more trips down to Rock Creek, the last one right at dusk. The days were long at this time of year, but the wounded kept on coming.

The sounds of gunfire finally stopped a few hours after dark. Exhausted, Rebekah and Beniah walked back to the main house. When he saw his mother carrying several loaves of bread out of the summer kitchen, he ran to her and hugged her. She twisted off two large pieces, one for each of them. Smiling, she said, "We heard you two did real well today. Mrs. Hovey came by earlier to get some bread for the surgeons and told me that you were both down at Rock Creek, fetching water." Sitting down at the table to eat their bread, they returned as big a smile as they could manage. As soon as he was done with his bread, Beniah stood and said to Rebekah, "I 'll see you in the morning." With that, he turned and headed toward the door to his house.

Rebekah wasn't finished eating, but she walked back to the Hovey wagon through the rows of treated men, most of whom were sleeping now. Wearily, she climbed up into the wagon and curled up behind the seat. She realized she hadn't seen Lieutenant Cunningham all day. Well, perhaps Beniah gave him water. She hoped he had. Her eyelids felt like stone, and she fell asleep before she could finish her bread.

Chapter 10
July 3, 1863, Before Dawn
The Battle Becomes Clear

In what seemed like a blink of an eye, Rebekah woke up to the roar of cannons firing on the hill right behind her, on the corner of the Spangler farm closest to Gettysburg. She poked her head out and saw flashes of cannon fire across Baltimore Pike. One of the men sleeping near the wagon sat up and asked in fright, "Is it the Rebs, is it the Rebs?"

A man lying nearby replied, "No, it's ours. They're trying to take back the part of Culp's Hill that we lost last night. I lost my hand trying to hold it."

Rebekah looked down at him. Compared to many of the others, he seemed so composed, so accepting that he had lost his hand. In the gathering light she saw that his uniform had the same markings as those of Lieutenant Cunningham and Lieutenant Barker, meaning he was a lieutenant as well. She rolled back into the space behind the seat and started to eat the bread she had left from last night. She listened as the lieutenant talked to the surrounding men.

"On the first day, they attacked from the west, up the Chambersburg Pike. Buford's cavalry held them off until the Iron Brigade came up, in the nick of time. They took terrible casualties. Eventually they got driven back through town, along with the 11th Corps from the north of town. But we held the high ground south of town.

"The Rebs have been trying to take Culp's Hill, on our right flank, for two days, and last night, they captured a section of it, but we will take it back this morning. Their major action yesterday was against our left flank, but it held. At the end of the day, they tried to flank the hill on our far left, a rocky mound called Little Round Top, but we held it. I sure hope we stay where we are because our entire line is above theirs."

The other men listened and offered their thoughts. For all they had been through, after being wounded and maimed, they all desperately wanted to see the Union win this battle and the war. As Rebekah listened to them from her hidden position behind the seat of the wagon, she pondered what this lieutenant was saying and what Lieutenant Cunningham had said about the Iron Brigade arriving just in time. She remembered that General Wadsworth had said that the Rebels would not be eager to see the Iron Brigade. She felt a deep sense of satisfaction, knowing that she had played a part in the Iron Brigade getting to Gettysburg when they did.

If the Union wins this battle, and wins the war, then slavery will end. Amos, Hannah, and Moses will be free!

But she also understood the cost of it all. In the past two days she had helped hundreds of wounded men, and perhaps helped save some lives. She hoped there would be no more fighting today, no more wounded, no more mutilated men being dropped off at the Spangler farm for medical care. She prayed as fervently as she ever had in her life, "Dear loving God, please let this end soon! And take me back to my family."

But from what the soldiers were saying, the battle had not been decided yet. They clearly expected more fighting to occur that day.

One added, "With Sedgwick's corps all here now, we'll outnumber them wherever they attack. That is, if we stay on the high ground."

Rebekah's thoughts were interrupted when Beniah climbed up into the wagon, proclaiming "Good morning!" Rebekah marveled at how strong and confident he now sounded. She remembered that a day ago he had seemed unable to do much of anything. "My mom sent you this breakfast." It was a piece of fresh bread with blackberries baked in and some beef jerky. "She told me, as soon as you eat, we need to get back to giving men drinks of water. It's going to be boiling hot today." Rebekah gazed at the sun rising in a cloudless sky in the east, just across Baltimore Pike, and she had to agree.

The wounded began arriving at the Spangler farm at a slower pace on that day, the third day of the battle. But the pace of work did not slow at all. The surgeons were busy addressing not only the new arrivals, but also wounded men who hadn't been considered critical when they first arrived. As Rebekah and Beniah made their water rounds, it seemed like they could never bring enough. The heat of the day did not help, but since the top of the barn and the other buildings were already full of wounded men, all the medical staff could do was lay the wounded out in the sun. Rebekah and Beniah ran into Mrs. Hovey in the top of the barn, and she encouraged them to keep the water flowing. She said the Army had a lot of tents and other badly needed supplies on the way, but they had not arrived yet.

"Are you okay, Rebekah? Are you tired?" Rebekah told her no, but they both knew she was fibbing. No one could be okay working in such heat and stench, among all these wounded and crying men. Plus, no one had gotten much sleep the last two nights.

Just then a soldier said, "Excuse me miss," as he backed into Rebekah. He was holding one end of a stretcher, on which a soldier was lying with a sheet pulled up over his face. Rebekah looked at Mrs. Hovey with sad eyes, understanding what that meant.

Mrs. Hovey, placing a hand on her shoulder, said softly, "Rebekah, when you come to a poor boy who has died, just close his eyes and move on. Someone will take him to be buried."

As the sun rose, the heat and humidity became oppressive. The calls for water by the wounded men grew louder and more insistent, and Rebekah and Beniah could not keep up. The one good thing was that the gun fire was decreasing, which meant fewer wounded men would be on their way.

But that changed in an instant early in the afternoon, when it seemed the entire world suddenly exploded in a horrific, ear-splitting noise! The Union cannon crews that had been parked on the fields of the Spangler farm closest to the fighting instantly hitched their horses to the cannon wagons and rode in the direction of the deafening noise.

Rebekah was terrified when a Confederate shell suddenly landed on the barn. She froze, and so did Beniah. But lots of men ran up from around the back of the barn and hurriedly started bringing wounded men out of the top of the barn. She saw Mrs. Hovey and Mrs. Spangler among them and instantly dropped her bucket and ran toward them. As she approached the barn door, she saw Mrs. Hovey leading a man who was leaning on her, hopping on the one leg he had left. "Rebekah, help us get these men out of the barn before the shells kill them!"

Repeatedly, Rebekah ran into the barn, helped a wounded man get to his feet and get out the door and up into the far field closer to Baltimore Pike, away from danger. The men leaned on her heavily, and several times she thought she would stumble and fall with a man on top of her, but somehow, she carried on. She wondered what her Mamm and Daed would think of her: head uncovered, dress filthy and torn, with semi-clad men draping their arms around her neck. "Surely, they're worried sick about me. I wish I could tell them I am alright."

Just as they finished clearing the top floor of the barn, freshly wounded started to come in on ambulances from the direction of the cannon fire. Rebekah and Beniah made several trips down to Rock Creek to refill their water barrels, but they could not keep up with the wounded who were pouring in. Because the fighting was so close, the ambulance trips back and forth from the battle to the farm were shorter, and there seemed to be an endless stream of screaming, pulsating, wounded men hurriedly unloaded by the ambulance crews.

Some of the less severely wounded were now limping in by themselves, while others were being helped by their comrades. One older soldier, a big, burly man, carried a smaller man in his arms. He approached Rebekah, crying, "My son, my son—please help him!"

Speechless, Rebekah turned and found a doctor who was examining some of the men who had just come in. She pulled his arm urgently, and he came over, glanced at the young man in the arms of his father and bluntly stated, "Your son is already dead." Then he moved on to the next ambulance. The burly man's legs immediately collapsed, and he plunged to the ground, still desperately holding his son, his head falling hard onto the grass. His mouth was agape with grief.

Rebekah lifted her cup and gently poured water into his mouth, careful not to make him choke on it. Tears were streaming down her cheeks, tears that she thought had dried up from the horror of the last two days. Little did she realize that the day was only going to get worse. A lot worse.

When the cannon fire slowed, she heard the yells and screams of men on the hillside beyond the farm, a noise that was soon overwhelmed by the rap of rifle fire. She shuddered to think that each bang meant another bullet was flying towards a man, and that thousands of those bullets would find their mark.

The doctor examining the men as they were unloaded from the wagons realized that many of the wounded had received no attention in the field before being brought in. Looking about in vain for someone to help, he spotted Rebekah. "You, Amish girl, come here!" He turned and grabbed a sack of rolled bandages and took one out. He reached out for a soldier who was being helped off a wagon, his left arm dangling at his side, blood spurting into the air. Sitting him down, the doctor looked up at Rebekah and grabbed a bandage. "Pull back the uniform from the wound. If there is a hole in the skin, stick a little of the end of the bandage on the wound, then wrap it around tightly. You must stop the bleeding!"

Turning to a young soldier squirming in the grass holding his belly, his intestines spilling out, the doctor said, "If they have a wound like that, don't bother. They can't be saved." With that, he was off to the next wagon. Shoulders slumped, her legs weak, Rebekah slowly turned, gazing at the horror all around her. She heard the doctor yelling at her, commanding her: "Get busy, girl, these men's lives depend on you!"

Man after man, ambulance after ambulance, the carnage of war came directly at her. When she had finished with one sack of bandages, she looked around and found another. She felt her mind going numb.

She no longer looked at the men, only at their wounds. The noise of the fighting reached a crescendo around three o'clock. The intense firing seemed so close that twice Rebekah turned and looked to see if the Rebels had broken through. She remembered what Lieutenant Cunningham had said to her on the first day of the battle, that on Chambersburg Pike that morning the Rebels kept coming until they did break through.

Suddenly an ambulance full of wounded men came speeding up so fast that the horses nearly trampled some of the men lying on the ground. Rebekah realized the driver was slumped over and had dropped the reins. The terrified horses had run back to where they were used to running but in their panic they weren't stopping. A few men instinctively ran up beside the lead horse and grabbed his harness. "Slow down, old boy, slow down." The horses stopped galloping, but pulled on their reins, trying to get free of the men holding them. Rebekah ran toward the lead horse and with a smile put her hands on both sides of his head and said as calmly as she could, "It's okay, it's okay. You're fine, shhh."

As the lead horse settled down from Rebekah's soothing, the others in the team did as well, their sides heaving and nostrils flaring. She looked back to the front seat and realized the driver was slumped over, seriously injured and the man next to him unconscious. The third man of the crew, standing behind the seat, was frozen in a terrified stare. A doctor ran over and climbed up the side of the wagon to examine the men. "They were hit by shrapnel. Both these guys are dead!" Turning toward the wounded men in the back of the ambulance, he said, "We'll get you off now, you'll be all right." As the men stepped off the back of the wagon, Beniah ran over and gave them a drink. Rebekah continued to hold the reins to keep the agitated horses still. The orderly helped hand down the two dead men off the seat to another man on the ground, then climbed back up and talked to the third man, who had not moved. He was white with fear and was visibly shaking. The orderly was talking to him, nodding his head at what the shocked man said. Then he jumped down, and looking around, he motioned for Rebekah and Beniah to come to him. "You two have been driving the water wagon the last couple of days, right?"

A bit apprehensive, Rebekah answered quietly, "Yes."

"Then the two of you get on the ambulance and go to the battle and bring back wounded. There are men dying on that field that need care immediately." Rebekah gaped at him, speechless. Beniah just blinked and looked to her for directions. The orderly crouched down so his face was level with hers and Beniah's, and looking back and forth, said to them, "Listen, I know you're just kids. You shouldn't have to see any of this. And I wouldn't ask you if there was anyone else. I am the closest thing to a doctor at this point, so I must stay here." Turning and pointing to the ambulance, he continued, "A shrapnel shell exploded right above them, killing two of them and now the third one is totally spooked out. But he can carry a stretcher. Can you two do this for me?" Then turning and pointing to where the battle was raging, he asked, "Can you do it for the men dying on that field?"

Rebekah could only manage to nod. Turning to Beniah, she signaled him to get on the ambulance. Although the fire had slowed in the last few minutes, the sounds of battle made her heart pound as she climbed up and sat beside him. To her surprise, the horses responded to Beniah's direction, and they obediently followed the wagons in front of her. They drove down the road past the schoolhouse and up the hill toward the sounds of the fighting. As they approached the top of the hill, the carnage of battle scene exploded into full view. As far as she could see to the left and right, soldiers in blue formed a line on top of a ridge, firing down at the retreating Confederates. For three days she had heard men talk about "good ground," and now she understood exactly what they meant. From the top of the ridge she was on, she could see the Confederates retreating across the valley below her and up the other side, many of them carrying wounded comrades. The ground between the retreating Rebels and the blue line appeared to be moving. Sucking in her breath, Rebekah realized that the movement she was seeing was actually Rebel soldiers squirming in agony, some trying to crawl back to their lines. There were hundreds, even thousands, of them in front of her. Her mouth was agape, in shock at the enormity of the horrific carnage. An officer yelled at her, snapping her back into reality. "Turn that ambulance around right here!"

As Beniah turned it around so the back of it was facing the soldiers, men came and grabbed the stretchers on the wagon, running off and quickly returning with wounded men on two of them. Then several soldiers, including an officer, ran up with a Confederate they were carrying in a blanket. "This is General Armistead; he's a friend of General Hancock!" they exclaimed. "Get him to a surgeon right away!"

The officer jumped on the back of the wagon as Beniah snapped the reins. When they got back to the farm and Beniah pulled the wagon around to where the men were being unloaded, Rebekah heard the officer who had stayed with the Confederate in the back of the ambulance shout to the doctor, "This is General Armistead. We need help immediately!" As soon as they handed down the stretcher, the doctor examined his wounds. "You should be all right, General," he said, and with that, the man in gray was taken to the surgeons at the barn.

Rebekah and Beniah made two more trips to the battlefield before the doctor told her that she would now be of greater use making sure the men had water. The fighting had stopped for now, and the number of newly wounded began to slow as well. But the afternoon was oppressively hot and humid. "There's no use to bring the wounded here if we have no water for them," he said. "They will die without it!" So, Rebekah grabbed Beniah and once again they headed off to Rock Creek.

Eventually the flow of wounded did stop. Many of the late arrivals were Confederates, men who just a few hours earlier had been trying to kill the very men who were now giving them medical aid. As Rebekah kneeled beside a wounded Confederate, she held his head up with one hand and poured water into his mouth with the other.

The man lying behind her reached up and weakly pulled at her arm. She was used to this by now; all these men were parched, but she could only give water to one man at a time. Automatically dipping the cup in the bucket of water, she turned to him and gasped when she saw his face. It was Lieutenant Barker, the first Confederate she had seen, four days ago! His face was almost white, and despite the heat, he seemed to be shivering, which she knew was a bad sign. As she gently gave him a drink, she turned her head and shouted for the doctor. He came over as she poured the last of the water onto his dry lips. She didn't have to say a word to the doctor; he saw the concern on her face. He pulled the bloody cloth off Barker's belly and then gently laid it back down again. His eyes met Rebekah's, and he just shook his head. There was nothing he could do.

Once again, she remembered hearing her father recite scripture: "But I say unto you, love your enemies, bless them that curse you, do good to them that hate you, and pray for them."

When Rebekah turned back to look at Lieutenant Barker, their eyes met, and through her tears she said softly to him, "Think of your wife, think of your baby. You will see them again in Glory." She remembered how she had heard him pray a blessing for the food in the dining room of her house, and she knew he was a believer. His lips formed a slight smile and he weakly put his hand on hers. Then his face went blank. She knew what that meant. Tenderly reaching out with her fingers, she closed his eyes.

"Why did you come here? Why did you leave your wife, your child and your farm?" she whispered, knowing he could no longer hear her or answer her. On her knees, she found herself incapable of moving. Her shoulders sagged and her back collapsed. Troubling thoughts ran through her head. Was it her fault that all these men were dying and horribly wounded? She sat back on the ground beside him, burying her sweaty head in her dirty hands, weeping, and shaking. She thought of how scared she was of him when she first saw him riding his horse through Marsh Creek. But when he was with her in the barn, he seemed so nice.

Oh, this war is so terrible! she thought. *Why couldn't Lieutenant Barker be back at his farm in North Carolina with his wife and baby? Why did he come all the way to Gettysburg just to be killed? And what about all these other men, going back to their families without arms or legs, maimed for life?*

Rebekah found no answers in her silent anguish. She just sat and wept, oblivious to the mayhem around her. Then a hand rested softly on her shoulder. Looking up, she saw it was Beniah. "Rebekah, we are out of water. We need to go to the creek to get more." He said it in a soft and tender voice, but Rebekah couldn't help but notice the strength with which he said it. For two days she had been the strong one, the one who saw to it that they did what needed to be done. Now, looking up at him, she nodded silently, stood up, and followed him to the water wagon. She would have to think about all this later, when wounded men were not crying out for water.

Chapter Eleven
July 3, 1863, Evening
The Aftermath of Picket's Charge

It had seemed like the day would never end, the sun would never set, and the blazing heat would never subside. The ambulance deliveries slowed, but the surgeries at the barn did not. At dusk, Rebekah heard a woman calling her name. Looking around, she saw it was Mrs. Hovey. "Over here! Here I am!"

"Oh, thank God I have found you!" Mrs. Hovey replied as she walked over and around the wounded men on the ground to come in Rebekah's direction. "We need you at the barn. Everyone is exhausted. They have barely slept since we got here. Dr. Hovey asked me to find somebody to help, and I thought of you. We need you to help us now."

Rebekah had purposely stayed away from the lower part of the barn since they arrived on the first day of the battle. The screaming and the intensity of the anguish coming from the forebay were too much for her. But now Mrs. Hovey was holding her hand, leading her there. Her heart started beating a little faster. As they got closer, working their way through the soldiers rushing the wounded to the barn and other soldiers taking the treated men away, Rebekah thought of her brothers. Up ahead, right behind the barn, there was a pile of split wood. Looking at it through all the commotion, it seemed like someone threw a log through the air and it landed on top of the pile. "Mrs. Hovey, why is someone splitting wood at a time like this?"

"What? Nobody's splitting wood … Oh, Rebekah, that's not wood, that is a pile of the amputated limbs. That's what we do; we must remove the shredded flesh and shattered bone from around the wound or it will get infected, and the men will die. That's a pile of limbs we have cut off this afternoon." Rebekah's legs suddenly felt like jelly. She wanted to puke, but her stomach was too empty and her throat too dry. Mrs. Hovey turned and faced her. Putting her hands on her shoulders, she said, "Honey, I know this is a lot to ask of a young girl. But we have no one else. The number of wounded in the last three days has just overwhelmed us. But I have seen what you have done, and I know you can do this!"

Turning and again leading Rebekah by the hand, she led her to the table where Dr. Hovey was working. He was covered with blood, and it mixed with his sweat and just oozed off him. His hair was matted down with sweat, and his eyes had a deep, hollow look. He was almost unrecognizable from the smiling, confident man he had been when she first met him. Rebekah looked down and saw that the ground was soaked with blood too.

"Rebekah will have to help you. There is no one else," Mrs. Hovey announced.

Dr. Hovey shook his head. "She's just a little girl. This isn't right. I need a man, or at least an experienced woman!"

"She's all we have. She will have to be your helper. You know what she's been through. She's smart, she's tough"—she turned to Rebekah and put a hand on her shoulder—"and she's strong."

Dr. Hovey shook his head, but sighed, resigned to the fact that Rebekah was going to be his assistant. "Pick up that wet dressing," he said, pointing to a bucket of water with several large bandages floating in it. She picked up a bandage and handed it to him. "No, you must wrap the wounds after we perform the surgery. Frank and I will do the surgeries; you will do the wrapping. Look, let me show you how." He had just amputated a man's arm just above the wrist. He was still asleep from the chloroform. "You need to leave it a bit loose so the wound can drain," he instructed.

Rebekah was a quick learner, and she needed to be. The wounded men, some on stretchers, some hobbling in on their own feet, were lined up waiting for the surgery that would keep them alive. She saw the exhaustion on Dr. Hovey's face and on the faces of all the medical staff. Now she understood why she was needed. She tried to block out the stench and ugliness all around her and focused on helping the wounded survive.

As night passed midnight, some of the surgeons and orderlies left to find a bedroll or just dropped to the ground, totally drained. The surgeon working next to Dr. Hovey called out to him as he was preparing to amputate a shattered foot. His helpers had collapsed, and he was asking for Frank's assistance. Staring back with glazed eyes, Dr. Hovey just nodded yes. Without saying a word, Frank went to help the other surgeon. Dr. Hovey turned and looked at the line of wounded still waiting and asked Rebekah, "We have only a few left, can you do this?" Rebekah looked at the stretcher two soldiers had just placed on the table. It was a boy not much older than her, tears running down his face, holding the stump on his right arm. She replied to Dr. Hovey, "Okay, I'll stay."

With a slight smile, Dr. Hovey turned his eyes to the chloroform bottle on the table. Rebekah picked it up, along with the rag beside it. She poured a lot of the liquid on the rag, and, mimicking what she had seen Frank do, she held it tight over the boy's mouth and nose until he went limp. She then picked up a pair of scissors and cut off the rest of the boy's sleeve as Dr. Hovey examined the wound. Although someone had applied a tourniquet to the top of his arm hours before, the wound was still bleeding. Dr. Hovey stuck his fingers into the wound, feeling for pieces of shattered bone and torn, dead flesh. Then, setting the arm flat on the table, he said, "Hold it tight. I'll make the cut right here."

The entire time she had been helping him, she had purposely turned away during the actual cutting. But now she was holding the boy's arm down, with her face just inches from the wound. Dr. Hovey first used a sharp knife, running it around the arm in a series of circular cuts, careful not to cut off the skin at the bottom of the wound. Pulling the flesh off from around the bone, he reached for his saw and commanded, "Hold it tight now, Rebekah, hold it tight!" It didn't take long for him to saw off the shattered bone. When he was finished, he picked it up, and along with the cut-away flesh, threw it on the pile of limbs just a few feet away. He did it with no more thought than Rebekah had seen Mamm do when she cut off the tops of carrots and threw them in a bucket.

"Release the tourniquet, slowly!" When she did, the blood came oozing out of the veins and spurting out of the arteries. "Okay, tighten it up again." One by one, he pulled the veins and arteries out of the stub to make them tight and then tied them in a knot to stop the bleeding. "Release it again." When she did, he saw that one artery was still bleeding, and he grabbed it and told her to tighten the tourniquet again. After tying the last one, he folded the bottom skin of the boy's arm up over the wound and pulled it tight. "Hold it like this while I sew it up." When he finished sewing the wound, he turned and said to Rebekah, "Okay, apply the dressing while I go and see how the next one looks."

As she wrapped the boy's arm, the two soldiers who had carried him in walked back to each end of the stretcher, waiting for her to say the surgery was finished and the boy was ready to be removed from the table. Rebekah was conscious of them looking at her, with a sense of respect and honor. She was not used to boys looking at her that way. *You do not know how little I really know about all of this,* she thought, *and you have no idea how much I wish I was home in my bed.* She dressed the wound, and then she looked up and nodded. They then slid the stretcher under the boy's side, gently placed him on it, and took him away.

As soon as they left, Dr. Hovey led two men with another stretcher over to the table. "Set him here," he instructed. The two men who carried the stretcher were pleading with Dr. Hovey not to cut the foot off the wounded soldier on the stretcher, which was badly mangled, with bones sticking out in a grotesque way. "We're his brothers, and he has a wife and kids back home, and he needs both legs to work his farm!"

Dr. Hovey just shook his head and, displaying his sheer exhaustion, said curtly, "Do you think I want to cut it off? Do you think I want to stay up in the middle of the night to torment him? If this wound gets infected, he will lose his entire leg and perhaps even die! Now stand back and let me and this girl here save his life. We need to cut it off right above the ankle." By the time he was done talking, Rebekah had the bottle of chloroform ready, awaiting the signal from Dr. Hovey. Turning to her, he said, "Go ahead, Rebekah, let's get started."

This surgery was somewhat more complicated because there were two leg bones that needed to be cut. As they worked, tears streamed down the cheeks of the two brothers, who had retreated a few steps backwards. Glancing at them, Rebekah realized how many tears she had seen grown men shed in the past three days. Amish men always seemed so stoic. But she reminded herself, *they don't make war.* The thought occurred to her that if all men had to watch a brother, who was a father and a husband, have his foot cut off in the middle of the night, they would be less eager to make war. There were many aspects of the Amish life that Rebekah had questioned in her life, but at this moment, holding a man's leg down while the bottom of it was cut off, she couldn't think of any of them.

As the weeping brothers removed the stretcher, another stretcher was placed on the table. The wounded man was tall, and his knee was shattered. The bottom of the leg was hanging at a twisted angle, connected by just a little skin and muscles on the inside of the leg. Dr. Hovey looked at the wound, but before he could examine it closely, his knees weakened, and he stepped backwards and collapsed on a bench. "I can't go on. This is too much for human endurance." Looking up and down the forebay, Rebekah realized that all the other surgeons had already gone, too exhausted to continue. But there were no more wounded soldiers, either.

"Dr. Hovey, this is the last one. He's already pale. He won't last the night." Doctor Hovey looked up at her and with glazed eyes said, "Okay, if you can do it, I can do it, let's go."

Reaching down her hand, Rebekah helped him to his feet again. The stretcher bearers were already gone. Only Dr. Hovey and Rebekah remained. When the chloroform rag was applied and the trousers cut away, Dr. Hovey started his work. He seemed wobbly and shaky, but when it came time for him to cut the flesh away from the bone, he recovered and made quick, clean cuts. The bone was a big one and took a bit longer to cut through.

As Rebekah alternately tightened and loosened the tourniquet, she noticed that Dr. Hovey was having trouble seeing the veins and arteries that needed to be tied up. She knew the bleeding needed to be stopped quickly or the soldier would die. But Dr. Hovey was having trouble getting the last one tied. Losing patience, he shouted to her, "Get me the tenaculum, now!" Rebekah took her hands off the wounded man's leg and went to the small table where Dr. Hovey's instruments were. She had no idea which one to pick up. "It's the hook, grab the hook!" he yelled. Handing a tool with a hook on the end to him, she then watched him stick his hand up inside the wound and try to hook the tool around the artery. But he couldn't. With a sigh, he stepped back and handed Rebekah the instrument. "I can't see it. My eyes are shot. It's up to you; you need to quickly find it and tie it off." He was so drained his voice was emotionless. Rebekah had no choice. She grabbed the hook and used it to search around inside the man's wound to find the last artery. She found it and pulled it out with the hook. With the other hand, she tried to pinch it tight so she could tie it into a knot. But it slipped out of her fingers, and it spurted blood onto her face.

Rebekah wanted desperately to turn and run away. But then Dr. Hovey put his hand on her shoulder. "Come on, Rebekah, find it and tie it." This time she did not let it slip out, and she was able to complete the knot and stop the bleeding.

She helped Dr. Hovey seal up the wound, and they applied the wet dressing together. "Grab the other end of the stretcher," he mumbled. They lifted him, and he was quite heavy. "Let's just set him over here, Rebekah. Someone will get him in the morning."

With that, Dr. Hovey turned and walked toward the Spangler home to find a place to lie down for a few hours. As Rebekah turned to do the same, she heard the soldier they had just operated on, coming out of the anesthesia, ask for water. Turning back, she saw his imploring eyes and promised to bring him a drink. Finding a bowl, she dipped it into the bucket where the wet dressings were and filled it. She walked to him and knelt. She lifted his head and slowly poured the water carefully into his parched mouth. When she was done, his lips formed a slight smile, and he fell into a fast sleep. Rebekah left him and turned back to the forebay.

Each step felt like she was carrying a huge stone, and her legs ached with exhaustion. She dropped the bowl in the bucket and slowly surveyed the scene. The hundreds of dying fires illuminated thousands of men lying on the ground, hundreds already dead. The Spangler house seemed like the place to go, but it was too far away. Turning into the barn, stepping over the men lying inside, she spotted a corn crib, too small for a man to lie in. She squeezed in and collapsed into the corn. Her head wedged into a corner; she instantly fell asleep.

Chapter Twelve
July 4, 1863, Morning
The Aftermath of War

When her eyes opened, the sun was well up in the sky. The barn floor was covered with men, most missing an arm or leg, and in some cases, both. Men were walking around giving them water. A doctor was walking through them, checking their wounds. He ordered a few of them to be taken back out to the forebay, to be worked on again. Rebekah unfolded herself from the corn crib and stood up stiffly. It had seemed a lot bigger last night when she collapsed into it. She was sore, but she had to get moving, as she badly needed to relieve herself. Walking toward the Spangler house, she saw dozens of men relieving themselves in long trenches, but quickly turned away. She made her way to the outhouse behind the Spangler home. When she was finished, she looked for Mrs. Hovey and found her in the summer kitchen, feeding the Spanglers and the orderlies.

When she saw Rebekah, she smiled and came over to her. Reaching her arms around her, she squeezed Rebekah and gently rocked her back and forth. Without releasing her, she said, "You really outdid yourself last night. Dr. Hovey said you did well, saved a lot of lives." When she released her, Rebekah looked up at her with tears in her eyes. She had been through so much, but in the arms of Mrs. Hovey, with her proud face smiling down at her, she knew it was worth it. Then she thought of her own mother, how she must be worried sick about Rebekah, and her tears flowed faster. She found an empty spot on the bench and sat down at the table. She ate her fill, surprising herself by eating a full second helping. She was eating a grown man's breakfast, but she reminded herself how hard she had worked the last few days, and how little she'd had to eat. As she was finishing, Beniah came over to her and smiled.

"Can you help me with water again? I had trouble with the horses again when I took the wagon down to Rock Creek this morning. A soldier had to help me out." Out of the corner of her eye, she saw Mrs. Hovey nodding to her.

"We should have enough help with the surgeries today, and there is more help arriving. But the wounded men who are in the fields will need water, lots of it. Make them as comfortable as possible. We still don't have the tents to set up for them, and it feels like rain coming."

Beniah and Rebekah spent the rest of the morning and early afternoon giving the wounded water and any comfort they could. The men's spirits were up because it was the fourth of July, and there was no more fighting. There were still ambulances arriving with wounded men, many of them Confederates. Word had it there was a truce so each side could pick up their dead and wounded.

As the afternoon arrived, the Confederates stopped coming out for their wounded. On the Union line, there was shouting because the Confederates were leaving, retreating back to Virginia. No matter how badly the men in blue were wounded, they greeted this news with pride and elation. As she was going up and down the rows of wounded, Rebekah had to wake a young officer. She told him the news of the Confederates leaving, and he was ecstatic. Unable to lift himself up because his left leg had been amputated below the knee, he clapped his hands and said to the men around him "Finally, finally, we had the good ground. No more Chancellorsville, no more Fredericksburg! And now, Bobby Lee is running back to Virginia with his tail between his legs!"

As Beniah steered the wagon back onto the Spangler farm from a trip to get water from Rock Creek, she saw Lieutenant Cunningham waiting for her. His left hand was bandaged, and he had his arm in a sling, but he was smiling. "You've been busy, Rebekah. I have noticed you the last couple of days and this morning, when I went looking for you over at the house, the good doctor's wife told me what you did last night." He paused, smiling at her as she smiled back at him, and added, "This is a lot more than you thought you were getting yourself into when you snuck out of your house, isn't it?"

With the way he smiled at her, and after what she had seen in the last few days, after what she had done the last few days, she knew she would never be a "little girl" again. She no longer needed to wonder when she would grow into a woman; she already had.

"But listen," he said as the smile left his face. "The Confederates are retreating, and I am recovering. You stay here and keep on helping, and just as soon as I can, I will get you back to your family. They must be plumb frantic about you."

Nodding, she turned and signaled Beniah and he snapped the reins, driving the wagon forward with more water, more water for men wounded and dying and much in need of that water. But she turned and looked back and saw Lieutenant Cunningham still smiling at her. She smiled back as she turned away. She felt a feeling inside, one she had never experienced. She did not understand it, but these past few days had changed her, and there was no going back.

Although the wounded were still being brought in, and the surgeons were busy under the forebay of the Spangler barn, at least there was no more gunfire, no more fighting, no more killing.

But in the late afternoon they heard thunder. At first, she feared it was more cannon fire, but soon the first raindrops began to fall. Rebekah looked around the fields with thousands of men lying out in the open. Mrs. Hovey had talked about tents at breakfast, but Rebekah saw none. A feeling of foreboding came over her. "Beniah, we have to get these men out of the rain."

"I bet we can get more inside the barn," he said. "I'm not sure if the top of the barn has been filled back up since we emptied it out yesterday when the cannonballs were landing so close by."

"You're right, Beniah, let's start with that!" They ran to the top of the barn and helped as many men as they could to get inside. Two orderlies were already in the barn instructing the men to squeeze in tightly. If they could sit rather than lie down, they did, creating space for more men. Once the barn was full, they tried to move other wounded men under wagons or into wagons that had covers. But most would have to stay out in the open.

"Where are the tents? Why don't they have any tents here?" Rebekah wondered aloud. They did the best they could for the men in the open, moving them out of the parts of the field that had water flowing through it to ground that at least wasn't as wet. Providing water and food as best they could they worked up and down the rows of men. For many, it was not enough. The dead were taken by orderlies down to the bottom fields, where they were quickly buried. The numbers were simply staggering. Rebekah and Beniah looked through the rain toward the lower fields. Dozens of men were digging graves. They stood and stared in anguish.

Snapping out of it, Rebekah grabbed Beniah by the shoulders. "Most of them are still alive, and we need to do what we can to keep them alive!" At that point, there were about two thousand wounded men at the Spangler farm. Rebekah and Beniah did their best to provide whatever cover they could, including, for some, stretching a blanket over a couple of upright sticks stuck in the mud.

When the rainfall stopped well after dark, they made their way back to the Spangler farmhouse. Some of the orderlies and surgeons were eating in the summer kitchen, so they sat down and ate with them. The fire was burning hot under the kettles of stew, and Rebekah sat next to it. She was soaked to the skin, and even after the intense heat of the previous days, she was cold. Mrs. Hovey was showing some new women who had come to the Spangler farm to help how the kitchen was set up. Rebekah was relieved to see so many women arriving. She had no intention of not doing what was needed, just as she had since the battle began, but she really wanted to go home. She thought of seeing her family, sleeping in a warm, dry bed, but most of all, eating her Mamm's cooking. She had overheard many of the wounded men talk about how they wanted to eat their mother's cooking and thought: *I guess I am not very different from them after all.*

General Armistead was sitting on the floor of the summer kitchen, propped up into a corner. To Rebekah, he looked like a grandfather, a very nice and polite man. But he was a man who, she presumed, held slaves. For years, ever since she had met the abolitionist in Cashtown, she had believed that all people who held slaves must be mean and wicked. But General Armistead did not seem mean and wicked.

When Rebekah had traveled into Cashtown over the years, or been in the company of English, she had come to know that they thought the Amish were rather strange. With these thoughts running through her mind, she silently shook her head. To her, what was strange was nice, polite men like General Armistead owning slaves.

When she was finished eating and reasonably dry, she walked tentatively toward Mrs. Hovey. She was shy to ask, but she really wanted to sleep in the house tonight. She did not have to ask. Mrs. Hovey looked at her and instantly knew what she wanted. Smiling, she put her arm around Rebekah and led her out of the kitchen, across the backyard and up the front porch and into the house. It was nice to be in a house, a real house, but although Rebekah was not expecting a neat and clean home like she was used to, the filth and stench inside the Spangler home shocked her. Wounded men lay all over the entire first floor, although most of them were older men, the officers. Mrs. Hovey hugged Rebekah and, with an acknowledging smile, led her up the stairs. She saw Beniah in one room, crammed in with the rest of his family. Mrs. Hovey led her into a room where Dr. Hovey and Frank were already lying down, sound asleep. Mrs. Hovey gestured to a blanket on the floor where they could both sleep, with Rebekah against the wall. It was no bed, but it sure beat the barn or the wagon, and Rebekah lay down to her first good night's sleep in days.

Chapter Thirteen
July 5, 1863, Morning
A General Dies and Help Arrives

The day brought both good and bad news. Rebekah woke up to learn that Confederate General Armistead had died overnight. It was only two days ago that she helped bring him to the Spangler farm in the ambulance. The night before, he had looked a lot better than many other wounded men, men who were still living. She imagined him living comfortably in a nice home in Virginia and wondered if he regretted coming this far to fight a war and be killed.

At breakfast in the summer kitchen, Dr. Hovey said that since the 11th Corps was leaving to follow the retreating Confederate Army, many of the surgeons and orderlies would have to go with them, to be ready to treat men wounded in another battle. But he was going to remain at the Spangler farm, to continue with the amputations and care for the wounded as they battled to recover. Mrs. Hovey said that with so much work to do, she too would stay as long as necessary.

The good news was that many women from the surrounding area were on their way or already there, eager to help. Plus, the tents so badly needed were to arrive later in the day. From the conversation she had overheard while eating her porridge, Rebekah had learned about the impending arrival of the Sanitary Commission and the Christian Commission, which she gathered from the conversations around the table, were volunteer organizations that had a lot of medical supplies.

Rebekah wondered why an army that had so many soldiers, so many horses, so many cannons, did not have enough food and medicine for the wounded. But as breakfast ended, they all went to work. She asked Mrs. Hovey if, since there were so many others ready to help, they could work together. "Yes, it will be great to have you with me. There will be enough orderlies and volunteers now to help the surgeons and get the water. You and I will clean the wounds of the men already treated, make sure the men get what they need, and help them write letters to their folks back home."

The farm changed so much that day. The cannons and all the battle-fit men and horses that worked them were gone. So was the headquarters and all the bustle involved with that. In fact, all the unwounded soldiers had left. *Off to fight another horrible battle!* Rebekah thought. But there was no time to dwell on that. The ambulances were busy in the morning bringing in wounded left behind by the Confederates when they retreated. Although many of them had been treated to a certain degree already, the surgeons were still busy performing amputations and cutting out dead flesh.

The tents did arrive, and men started to put them up in neat order. At last, the wounded men would at least be under cover from the sun and rain.

Rebekah and Mrs. Hovey began their day in the barn, where most of the men were severely wounded. They cleaned them up, helped them eat, and changed some of their clothes if clean ones were available. Rebekah was amazed at how well Mrs. Hovey could comfort them. She encouraged them and prayed for them if they wanted her to. When she prayed, she would lay a hand on the wounded soldier she was praying for. Soon Rebekah was doing the same.

Many of the men spoke very little English. "The 11th Corps includes a lot of German immigrants," Mrs. Hovey explained. But to her delight, she found out that Rebekah could speak to them in German! Her Amish dialect was different from the German these men spoke, so she didn't understand everything they said, but she bridged the gap and was able to get the addresses of their loved ones and to communicate what the wounded men were trying to say to their loved ones back home.

Mrs. Hovey often ministered to their spiritual needs. She asked them if they loved the Lord Jesus Christ. Many said they did, and she encouraged them to believe that if they succumbed to their wounds, they would live with Jesus in heaven. If the men did not profess to know Jesus as their Lord, and they were willing, she would lead them in a statement of faith. Rebekah was part of a community that lived according to their faith, but she had never seen anyone so boldly profess their belief to so many strangers. As Rebekah and Mrs. Hovey left a wounded man to move on to the next one, Rebekah often looked back and noticed a look of peace on the faces of men Mrs. Hovey had prayed for.

In the afternoon, they returned to the kitchen and had a bowl of soup and fresh baked bread. It was the first real lunch Rebekah had enjoyed in almost a week. As they were finishing, Dr. Hovey walked over from the barn. Although exhausted, he wore a look of satisfaction and relief. "I believe we've completed most of the amputations. The ambulances have brought in many wounded from the abandoned Confederate lines. I'm sure we'll have to remove more limbs because of infection, but the worst should be over."

Rebekah gazed over the fields full of wounded men. "Thank God." She meant to say it under her breath, but the words came out.

"Yes, thank God! I pray now that we can give them the care they need to survive. These men are very weak and are still in grave danger." With that, Mrs. Hovey reached for Rebekah's hand and led her back to the care of the men.

In the later afternoon, as they approached a group of men putting up a tent, Rebekah recognized Lieutenant Cunningham. He was holding a stake in his bandaged hand and swinging a hammer with the other. Mrs. Hovey rushed to him and grabbed hold of the hammer as he had it raised to drive a stake. "You can't do that! You'll open the wound and get it infected! You could lose your entire hand and even die, like so many of the others down there being buried in the orchard.

My husband and others have worked tirelessly since we got here to keep men like you alive. Please don't make their efforts in vain!"

Standing, he looked at her and then at Rebekah. Nodding, he handed the hammer to a young man, a local farmer who was helping out. "Okay," he said, "you're right. I surely do appreciate all the efforts of everyone here, but there is so much to do!" Looking around the decimated farm and shaking his head, he murmured, "There is so much suffering."

"I know, but you have done your part. Now, promise me you will take it easy," Mrs. Hovey replied sternly.

He nodded and replied, "I will." Turning to Rebekah, he said, "The Rebels are all gone. As soon as I can get a horse, I'll take you home."

"Please get a wagon also," she replied.

He smiled, thinking back to the first night he saw her, and how he had been told that a young Amish girl would never be seen on the back of a horse with a strange man. Although she had ridden on the wagon and then the ambulance with the Spangler boy, Cunningham understood that she had only been doing what needed to be done at critical times and in front of military people, not Amish people. When he took her home, she would be seen by the Amish community and, most importantly, her father. He certainly did not want to cause her any discomfort.

"Okay, we owe you that at least," he promised.

Mrs. Hovey seemed taken aback. "You know each other?"

Lieutenant Cunningham replied, "She walked into our picket lines on the night before the battle. She has an abolitionist's zeal and snuck out of her house to tell us about the Confederate battle plans. I took her to Buford, then to Reynolds' headquarters. She's the reason the Iron Brigade came up so fast on the first day. "

Mrs. Hovey was thinking, putting everything together. "Then later, in the middle of the night, they brought her to us, to our tent." Turning to Rebekah, she said, "You have had quite the ordeal these last few days." She stroked Rebekah's hair and, looking at Lieutenant Cunningham, added: "Please see to it that you find a way to get her back home, but do not hurt that hand! Get somebody to help with the horse and wagon."

"Yes ma'am, I will," he promised.

"You will what, get her home or take care of your hand?" Mrs. Hovey asked with a suspicious smile.

Lieutenant Cunningham nodded and chuckled. "Both, I promise."

Mrs. Hovey and Rebekah continued their work. Although there were so many other women, local women and women from the Sanitary and Christian Commissions arriving, the sheer magnitude of the suffering continued to push them to their limits. That night, after the sun set, Mrs. Hovey sat at the kitchen table and wrote letters to the families of some of the men she had treated that day. From her memory and her scribbled notes, she expressed to their families what the wounded men had said to her. Rebekah kept busy, helping Mrs. Hovey remember the details of what some of the German-speaking men had told them and with baking the bread. With about two thousand wounded men and now hundreds of people attending to them, the bread could not be baked fast enough.

Later that night, as Rebekah stood kneading the dough at the other end of the table, Dr. Hovey came in. Sliding onto the bench next to Mrs. Hovey, he put his arm around her. "Marilla, you have done great work these last few days."

"Oh, Bleeker, so have you! I shudder to think what would have happened to these poor men if you weren't here!" They shared a tender hug, with tears in their eyes. Her voice breaking, Mrs. Hovey added, "I wish this war would end. The suffering is unbearable!"

"I know, I know it is, Marilla, but I will stay with these boys as long as I am needed."

The emotion of the moment was too much for Rebekah. As she had done late the night when she was helping Dr. Hovey at the surgeon's table, she collapsed back into a chair and wept, her head in her hands. Out of the corner of her eye, she noticed Dr. Hovey, with Mrs. Hovey's head on his chest, wave her over. She ran around the table and squeezed as tightly as she could to the side of Mrs. Hovey. Rebekah had cried before, but never had she felt so much weight on her heart as she felt at that moment. Mrs. Hovey reached an arm around her, squeezing Rebekah tightly as Dr. Hovey squeezed them both.

After some time, they raised their heads, their cheeks streaked with tears. Dr. Hovey reached around the back of Mrs. Hovey and tenderly pulled the tear-soaked hair off Rebekah's face. Looking at her, he said, "The good Lord has not seen fit to give us a daughter. But I will always think of you as a daughter for Marilla and me in this most trying time." Pausing, and glancing at Mrs. Hovey and then back to Rebekah, he continued, "But I will not think of you as Rebekah, our little Amish girl. I will think of you as Esther. For truly, God has brought you here for such a time as this." Mrs. Hovey did not speak, but with her smile and embrace affirmed everything her husband had said.

The Book of Esther was Rebekah's favorite Old Testament book. Rebekah smiled as she thought about Esther and how she had saved so many of her people, and she was thankful that God had used her to help so many "in such a time as this." *But don't be prideful*, she reminded herself. Thinking of the Amish way brought her mind back to her family. What were they going through? How the worry and anguish must be weighing on them! *Soon*, she thought, *soon I will be going home.*

The battle was over, and there were not many more wounded being brought in. The last of the men who had been lying out in the open were finally being placed in some sort of shelter. People from the community, men and women from the Sanitary Commission and the Christian Commission, all joined in to help the exhausted 11th Corps medical staff. But the suffering was far from over. Many men had to be taken back to the forebay of the barn, to undergo more surgery. Many who had been suffering horribly for days from untreatable belly wounds finally died. Even the men who were improving were still in pain, and their wounds needed care. Even the simplest tasks, like eating or relieving themselves required help.

Rebekah noticed wagons heading toward Gettysburg and returning with medical supplies, blankets, and food. But people, lots of people, were still required to properly use those supplies to treat the wounds of the men, distribute the blankets, and prepare the food.. She saw Beniah working with his older brother, bringing water up from Rock Creek in the wagon that she and Beniah had used. He smiled down at her as they passed Mrs. Hovey and Rebekah. He seemed so much stronger now, so much older. The thought occurred to her that the two of them had matured several years over the last few days.

As busy as they were, Rebekah kept an eye out for Lieutenant Cunningham. She would continue to help in any way she could as long as she was on the Spangler farm. But she wanted to go home. As much as she had come to love and respect Mrs. Hovey, she wanted to be with her Mamm. She wanted to feel her Daed's arm around her, to eat her Mamm's cooking, to see her sisters and brothers, and to sleep in her own bed.

Chapter Fourteen
July 6, 1863, Afternoon
A Parting Recognition

In the middle of the afternoon, he finally came. Pulling up near where Mrs. Hovey and Rebekah were cleaning up a soldier who had been shot with a grazing wound to the head, Lieutenant Cunningham called out, "This nag ain't much, but she should get us a couple of miles down the Chambersburg Pike!" Mrs. Hovey and Rebekah stood up and looked at each other for a moment. It was time for Rebekah to go.

Looking into each other's eyes, they shared a silent moment of love and respect.

"We will miss you, Rebekah! You have been such a miraculous help."

With a slight smile, Rebekah asked softly, "You aren't going to call me Esther, like Dr. Hovey?" She again remembered the biblical Esther, the young woman who had found herself in a position she could never have imagined, in a place where she was able to save her people.

Laughing, Mrs. Hovey replied, "No, but I can't help believing that God in heaven brought you to us for such a time as this." She leaned forward and embraced Rebekah and gave her a soft kiss on her forehead.

Rebekah was too choked up to say anything more. She turned to the wagon and jumped up into the back. Lieutenant Cunningham tipped his hat to Mrs. Hovey and gently snapped the reins, and the horse started toward Taneytown Road. Rebekah looked out the back of the wagon toward Mrs. Hovey. They never took their eyes off each other until the wagon rounded a bend and the Spangler farm faded from sight.

The ride down Taneytown Road into Gettysburg was a stark reminder of the carnage that had taken place just a few days before. Destruction was everywhere! Neat fences were destroyed, trees shredded by cannon fire and bullets, and men were busy burying dead horses. Rebekah tried not to think of it. She'd had enough war. And now she was going home!

Pulling into Gettysburg itself, she couldn't help but note the noise and bustle. People were moving everywhere; all seemingly part of the relief effort. Finally, Lieutenant Cunningham turned the wagon left onto Chambersburg Pike. Looking up, she noticed the angle of the afternoon sun and knew she was heading in the direction of home. On the other side of town, to the North, there were more signs of battle, but soon they were heading down a slight grade away from Gettysburg, away from all the carnage. When they crossed the stone bridge over Marsh Creek, her heart began to beat in a different way.

She turned around in the wagon, facing forward now with great anticipation. She saw their barn first. Then she saw her house! There was no one on the front porch, but she could sense her family inside. She did not notice her brothers on the other side of the road, doing their best to repair the damage done by the Confederates to the chicken coop.

Zephaniah saw her first. He shrieked out as he ran across the road, "Mamm, Daed, Rebekah's home!" In a moment her Mamm came running out the front door onto the porch and jumped down the stairs. "Oh, thank God, thank God in Heaven! You're alive, you're safe!" she screamed. Daed ran from the other side of the house, still holding the hammer he had been using to repair a fence. "Liebchen, liebchen, are you alright? Did they harm you? We've been worried sick about you!"

As the wagon stopped in front of the house, Rebekah unlatched the wagon gate. Ezekiel was already there, waiting with a huge grin, reaching out his hand. She gladly accepted his help getting down and then ran to Mamm and Daed, bursting into tears of joy and relief. They hugged her, her Mamm in tears, her Daed all smiles, as Zephaniah and Ezekiel ran into the house to fetch their sisters. Then, noticing the blood and dirt on her clothes, her Daed asked again, "Rebekah, did they take you? Did they hurt you?"

"No, Daed, I'm fine, but I have a lot to tell you. I am so happy to be home!"

Lieutenant Cunningham turned the wagon around in the barnyard and steered it back towards Gettysburg. Rebekah, hearing the wagon moving, lifted her head off Mamm's shoulder and turned toward the lieutenant. He looked down at her and they shared a smile, a smile of deep respect and immeasurable thanks. Then Rebekah turned toward the front porch as Mamm led her away. Caleb Stutzman, with the instincts of a father, noticed the smile. Turning to Lieutenant Cunningham, he said warily, "English, remember, she is just a little Amish girl."

Lieutenant Cunningham, watching her walk up the porch steps with the all the events of the last week racing through his mind, replied, "No she's not. Not anymore, she's not."

LIST OF CHARACTERS

Ages in the summer of 1863

FICTIONAL

Rebekah Stutzman, 13, the little Amish girl
Caleb Stutzman, 42, her father
Emma Stutzman, 41, her mother
Ruth Stutsman, 17, her sister
Mary Stutsman, 16, her sister
Zephaniah Stutzman, Zeph, 10, her brother
Ezekiel Stutsman, Zeke, 9, her brother
Lt. Samuel Barker, Confederate States of America (CSA) Army 22
Lt. Tim Cunningham, Union (USA) Army 22
Elijah Summers, formerly enslaved man living with and working for
Mr. Mickley
Amos, enslaved man on abolitionist's pamphlet
Hannah, enslaved woman on abolitionist's pamphlet
Moses, enslaved boy on abolitionist's pamphlet

CIVIL WAR ARMY UNITS

Army: A large fighting group under one field commander. These were
typically named for the geographical region they fought in.
Corps: A group of several Army divisions. At the time of the Gettysburg
battle there were three Corps in the Confederate Army of Northern
Virginia and seven Corp in the Federal Army of the Potomac
Division: 2-3 in a corps
Brigade: 2-4 in a division
Regiment: 2-5 in a brigade

HISTORICAL FIGURES, CONFEDERATE STATES OF AMERICA (CSA) ARMY

General Robert E. Lee, Commander Army of Northern Virginia, 56
General Jubal Early, 2nd Division, II Corp, 47
General J.E.B. Stuart, Cavalry commander, 30
General A.P. Hill, III Corps commander, 38
General Henry Heth, Division commander in A.P. Hill's Corps, 38
General Johnson Pettigrew, Brigade commander in Heth's Division, 35
Colonial Henry Burgwyn, Regiment commander in Pettigrew's Brigade, 21
General James Longstreet, II Corps Commander, 42
General George Picket, Division commander in General Longstreet's Corps, 38
General Lo Armistead, Brigade commander in Picket's Division, 46

HISTORICAL FIGURES, UNITED STATES OF AMERICA (USA) ARMY

President Abraham Lincoln, 54
General George Meade, Commander Army of the Potomac, 48
General John Buford, Cavalry Commander, 37
General John Reynolds, in command of I, III and XI Corps of Union Army, 43
General James Wadsworth, 1st Division Commander, I Corps 56
General Solomon Meredith, Iron Brigade Commander in 1st Division 53
Dr. Bleecker Hovey, XI Corp Medical Corps, 44
Marilla Hovey, Dr. Hovey's wife and a volunteer nurse, 43
Frank Hovey, their son and an orderly, 17

NON-FICTIONAL CIVILIANS

Jacob Mickley, Innkeeper Cashtown Inn
George Spangler, Farm owner, XI Corps hospital, 47
Elizabeth Spangler, wife of George, 44
Harriet Spangler, 21
Sabina Spangler, 19
Daniel Spangler, 17
Beniah Spangler, 14

SYNONYMOUS TERMS FOR CIVIL WAR COMBATANTS

United States of America
The North
The Federals
Yankees
The Blue

Confederate States of America
The South
The Confederates
Rebels
The Grey

AUTHOR'S NOTE

About forty years ago on a Saturday night, I was sitting in front of our fireplace in Houston, Texas, with my wife and two young daughters. My wife Deby asked me to tell a story, so the kids would fall asleep. I love history and can talk about various aspects of it for hours. For whatever reason, I chose to talk about Gettysburg that night. I began by saying that for two years the Civil War had been raging and although the South was winning the battles, they were losing the war. To my surprise, my 6-year-old daughter Erin interrupted me and asked, "Dad, how can they be winning the battles and losing the war?"

Not wanting to get bogged down in a discussion of the logistics of 19th century armies or the industrial advantages of the North, I replied something to the effect of, "Well, we can talk about that when you are older."

But my wife Deby said, "No, David—she's smart, explain it to her."

So, I discussed the situation faced by the Confederacy and its top general, Robert E. Lee, in 1863. In the first two years of the war the South won most of the battles, at least the battles fought east of the Appalachian Mountains. But those battles were fought in Virginia, which was the largest state in the Confederacy. The effect of hundreds of thousands of men marching back and forth along with all their horses was devastating to the farms and towns of Virginia. Both armies "lived off the land," meaning that the men ate the produce and livestock of the farms and towns that were in their path, and their horses grazed the fields bare and drank the wells dry.

The Confederacy was also losing the war because they could not match the Northern production of iron, ships, wagons, ammunition, horses, and food. The economy of the South was based on their enslaved people producing cotton and tobacco, but those products were not what was necessary to fight a modern war. This problem for the Confederacy is poignantly pointed out by Rhett Butler in the opening scene of the movie *Gone With the Wind*. Each month that the war dragged on the South had fewer and fewer supplies and the North had more and more. In the summer of 1863, realizing that the current strategy of fighting a defensive war was untenable, Confederate General Robert E. Lee risked everything in an invasion of the North. His goals were to relieve the pressure on Virginia, capture or destroy as much of the North's industrial production as possible, and to convince the people of the North that continuing to fight the war was fruitless.

With this background information, I tried to make up a story that my two young girls, 6-year-old Erin and 4-year-old Lindsay, could understand and associate with. I also wanted the story to inspire them on a personal level, which would be difficult because all the soldiers in the Civil War were men. Lastly, I wanted to make sure they knew the Civil War was fought over the issue of slavery, not State's Rights, as they would surely have heard in Houston as they grew older. I made the protagonist an Amish girl because she would be the least likely person to influence what turned out to be a brutal, decisive conflict between 170,000 heavily armed men.

Since my stories often had the desired results of putting the girls to sleep, I repeated the story over the next few years, adding to it and changing it. The kids and Deby enjoyed the story, and I felt it was achieving the joint goals of telling history and instilling into my girls a sense of female empowerment. As I was busy in my career in the home-building industry and very committed to volunteer work, it took me a long time to write the story down, which I finally did in longhand. Years later my daughter Erin, the person I had largely patterned my main character on, typed it onto a computer disc.

In my story, after Rebekah completed her desired goal of informing the Union Army of Lee's plans to converge on Gettysburg, I needed to create a storyline of what she did from that point forward during the battle. She couldn't simply walk back to her family in broad daylight while the battle raged. In my initial draft, I had her end up in a supply unit, helping women prepare food. But that was boring. As I investigated the possibility that she helped in a hospital, I discovered that the National Park Service had recently purchased a run-down farm that had been used as the 11th Corps field hospital during the battle. Several years later, Deby and I toured the newly refurbished barn and the property on our sixth or seventh trip to Gettysburg. I was extremely fortunate to have available to me Ronald Kirkwood's wonderful book *Too Much for Human Endurance*, published in 2019. This exceptionally detailed book provided me with the setting where I placed Rebekah for the second half of the book.

She's Just a Little Amish Girl is first and foremost a work of fiction. My goal was to write a historical fiction book about Gettysburg that would appeal to adults interested in history and to also inspire young people. This book is not intended to be a rigorous non-fiction study of the battle. There are many wonderful books that are, and I have read several of them, perhaps most impactfully, the middle book of Bruce Catton's Army of the Potomac Trilogy, *Glory Road*. I also owe much of the theme of the battle having been a race to gain the high ground to Michael Shaara's 1974 book "The Killer Angles." The 1993 movie *Gettysburg*, inspired by this book, also does a great job of stressing the importance of the Army of the Potomac positioning themselves on the higher ground of Cemetery Hill and Cemetery Ridge.

While *She's Just a Little Amish Girl* is fairly accurate with respect to actual commanders and troop movements, as a writer of fiction, I've taken the liberty of altering or adding imaginatively to the facts of the battle. The most important change is that Union General James Wadsworth, commander of the First Division of the I Corps, is woken around 2 a.m. to hear Rebekah's report of the Confederate plan to attack Gettysburg in the morning. He then orders his division to march toward Gettysburg. According to historical records, Wadsworth's commanding officer, General John Reynolds, was woken at 4 a.m. by a courier carrying a letter from General Meade ordering Reynolds to get his troops on the road toward Gettysburg as soon as possible. I imply in my story that the two-hour head start is what enabled the leading brigade of the First Division, the famed Iron Brigade, to arrive on the field of battle in time to reinforce General John Buford's cavalry. Buford's men were engaged in a desperate struggle to slow down the much larger Confederate forces advance into Gettysburg until additional Union troops could arrive. In my book, the First Division is mobilized because First Lieutenant Tim Cunningham, a fictional character, believes Rebekah's report of the Confederate plans, and together they convince General Buford and finally General Wadsworth of the validity of Rebekah's report. This is what makes Rebekah a hero.

To many Americans, the Battle of Gettysburg is ancient history. They have heard of the battle, but don't understand it and the critical role it played in American history. I hope looking at the battle from the eyes of a 13-year-old Amish girl will help to fill in the gaps in their knowledge. I certainly believe it has helped in that regard with my daughters Erin and Lindsay.

One final footnote: the final words of the book are spoken by the fictional Union Lieutenant Tim Cunningham, who, after Rebekah's father sternly reminds him that she is 'just a little Amish girl,' replied, "No she's not, not anymore she's not."

I penned this line to leave open the possibility of a sequel, the theme which I am already working on. But this time, I won't take forty years to complete it.

I want to thank my wife and daughters, especially Erin, for their patience and advice on this book. I also am deeply indebted to my editor, Doreen Martens, who not only provided wonderful developmental editorial work but also educated me on many aspects of Amish life.

Finally, the National Park Service needs to be commended for the amazing job they do preserving and presenting the battlefield. Every time I visit, there are improvements and new ways to look at the battle that took place over 160 years ago. I encourage every reader to visit the battlefield, whether it is your first visit or the latest of many. There are so many impressive parts of the battlefield to take in, but I recommend every reader allow themselves enough time to visit the Spangler Farm. Stand beside the Spangler barn, close your eyes, and who knows? You may see a thirteen-year-old Amish girl scurrying through the rows of wounded men with a water pail.

THE HISTORICAL IMPORTANCE OF THE BATTLE OF GETTYSBURG

A reader may ask, "There have been so many battles in so many wars, why is Gettysburg so important?" An answer could be made that all battlefields are important, and they all are part of the fabric of war and therefore they are part of the world that we live in. None the less, Gettysburg does indeed stand out for several reasons. One is that the number of casualties was absolutely staggering, over 50,000 men wounded, taken prisoner, or killed during the three-day battle. Of that number, about 10,000 were killed or died from their wounds in the weeks following the battle. Secondly, the battle was such a pivotal turning point in the Civil War. Furthermore, since the men on both sides were American, their valiant actions in defense of what each side fervently believed in are forever forged into our national heritage.

As discussed in the author's note above, in the Summer of 1863 the Confederacy was as concerned about its strategic long-term future as it was proud of its victories in the first two years of the war. The Union Navy's blockade of its ports, the success of General Grant and the Union army west of the Appalachians and the overwhelming industrial and agricultural production of the North threatened the long-term viability of the Confederacy. Against this backdrop, General Lee believed a bold move was required, and like a player of the modern board game of Risk, he gambled the future of Confederacy on an invasion of the North. In June of 1863, Lee snuck his Army of Northern Virginia across the Blue Ridge Mountains and marched north up the Shenandoah Valley, leaving Richmond unprotected. The Union Army of the Potomac did not know where they were and how fast they were moving, but since its primary function was to protect Washington, the troops stayed put in their camps across the Potomac River from the capital. Only when they realized how fast and how far Lee was moving did they break camp, cross the Potomac and follow him north.

As Lee moved north, he could not keep all his army moving together. He separated them, with different corps and divisions following different routes at different times. He did this so the farms, fields, and wells in his path would not be decimated by the leading units, leaving nothing for the following units. The risk of this strategy was that if the Army of the Potomac consolidated itself first, while his units were spread out, they could defeat the units of the Army of Northern Virginia one by one. Lacking modern surveillance tools like radar, airplanes, or satellites, the armies depended on spies and their cavalry units to let them know where the enemy was. A central part of the Gettysburg story is that the leader of the Confederate cavalry, J.E.B. Stuart, a flamboyant, sometimes egotistical leader, decided to ride farther east than Lee expected him to. Instead of operating between the two armies and keeping tabs on the Army of the Potomac for Lee, he rode his men to the far side of the Union Army, losing touch with Lee.

Lee's lack of definitive knowledge of the Union Army's whereabouts, and a spy's reports that the Army of the Potomac was indeed following him north quicker than he'd initially believed, led to Lee's decision to consolidate his troops in the last days of June. He initially chose Cashtown, Pennsylvania for the meeting point and began to move the main portion of the Army of Northern Virginia over South Mountain from Chambersburg to Cashtown on Chambersburg Pike. Then, realizing that many of the roads his units would need to travel on converged eight miles to the east in Gettysburg, he changed his plans and ordered them to consolidate there instead. Because he had scant knowledge of where the opposing troops were, he ordered his commanders to avoid a heavy battle until all his units arrived in Gettysburg.

Civil War battles were based much less on rapid movement of troops than modern warfare, with all its mechanized capabilities. The tactic in the Civil War was for an army to mass its troops tightly together to create a dense battery of fire, and to boldly march against a smaller mass of troops. The outcome of this type of fighting always favored the larger army and the army that was on higher ground. Firing down on men marching uphill is much more devastating than firing upwards at troops on top of a hill. Essentially, the Battle of Gettysburg was a race to see which side could get the most troops to Gettysburg first to claim the high ground and make their enemy attack them.

General George Meade, whom President Lincoln appointed commanding general of the Army of the Potomac just days before the battle, delivered one of my favorite quotes. When the battle started on July 1, he was far to the south of Gettysburg, but receiving reports that a major battle had broken out, he rode long and hard on an extremely hot day and arrived at the Union headquarters sometime around midnight. Always ornery and often profane, he is said to have walked into the house that his generals on the field had chosen as their headquarters, and without a polite hello or military salutation, snarled, "I hope the hell this is good ground." General Hancock, second in command of the Army of the Potomac, replied, "Yes sir, this is good ground, this is very good ground." Indeed, it proved to be just that.

History records that lead elements of the Army of the Potomac did get to Gettysburg in time to hold off the larger Confederate units descending from the west and north of town long enough to allow Union reinforcements to take up defensive placements on the higher Cemetery Hill and Cemetery Ridge south of town. This stellar defensive position was recognized the day before the battle by General Buford, who then in turn recommended it to General Reynolds when he arrived in Gettysburg on the morning of July 1. At that point, before his death just minutes later, Reynolds sent orders to General Olliver Howard, commander of the next-to-arrive XI Corps, to push his lead elements to the north of town but to have one of his divisions remain on Cemetery Hill on the south side and establish a fallback defensive position.

What makes Gettysburg such a fascinating part of history is the condensed timetable of the battle and its huge ramifications as the turning point of the war. Saratoga is often noted as the turning point of the Revolutionary War, but that battle was fought was four years before General Cornwallis surrendered his troops at Yorktown, and the

Americans suffered many setbacks in between, particularly in the south. During WWI the American Army helped the French and English turn back the German Spring offensive in the summer of 1918, but the tide of the war took months of hard fighting along a front hundreds of miles long to finally turn. In WWII, the British turned back the Germans at El Alamein and the Russians defeated the Germans at Stalingrad, but those battles lasted weeks and months. In comparison, the decisive turning point of the Civil War took place at a specific time at a specific place. The time was approximately 3 p.m. on July 3, 1863, and the place was at a Union cannon battery where two stone walls came together at a right angle in the middle of the Union position, which stretched along Cemetery Ridge from Culps Hill to Little Round Top. This was near the "copse of trees" that General Lee reportedly pointed to as the aiming point of the final attack, which we know as Picket's Charge.

At the decisive point of the raging fury, Confederate General Armistead led about 1,500 troops in a desperate final charge to break the Union line. It is said that he led his men so deeply into the Union lines that he had actually placed his hand on a captured Union cannon, in hopes of turning it on the Union troops, when he was dropped by three bullets. This point is known as the High Watermark of the Confederacy. After they were forced back from that point, the Confederates never again had enough men and material to launch a large-scale offensive. The tide of the Civil War changed at that moment.

If the Confederates had been successful at this point, this nation's history and probably world history could have been much different. Lee's Army of Northern Virginia might have continued to Harrisburg and perhaps even to Philadelphia. The strategic losses to the Union would have been catastrophic, and perhaps led to Northern public opinion turning against the war and against Abraham Lincoln, who was up for re-election a year later. If the Confederates won at Gettysburg and preserved the Confederacy, the United States would have been broken into pieces, much like Latin America. California could have led a western nation, and Texas could have formed its own Republic again.

Without the presence of a strong United States of America, the outcomes of both World Wars in the 20th century could have been much different.

As it was, the defeat at Gettysburg was the beginning of the end for the Confederacy. The next day, Union General Ulysses Grant captured Vicksburg, and the North gained control of the Mississippi River. Although their final defeat came two years later, at Appomattox in Virginia, the fate of the Confederacy was sealed at Gettysburg.

Another fascinating aspect of the Battle of Gettysburg is the plethora of "what ifs". "What if" General Stuart had attended better to his duties of reporting Union troop movements to General Lee? Lee could have had a better opportunity to pick the place for the decisive battle. "What if" General Heth had been more obedient to Lee's order to avoid a general battle until all his forces could be consolidated? Perhaps the bulk of Lee's Army of Northern Virginia could have arrived on July 1 and then captured Cemetery Ridge the next day, before the Union realized that Lee had consolidated his troops. "What if" General Ewell had interpreted Lee's order to take Cemetery Hill "if practicable" differently? The Confederates would have held the high ground for the rest of the battle. "What if" Union General Gouverneur Warren had not recognized and corrected the tactical blunder of the Army of the Potomac of not putting troops on Little Round Top on July 2? The Confederates could have taken the hill and fired their cannon down on the Union lines. "What if" General Lee had listened to his second in command, General James Longstreet, and pulled away from Gettysburg after most of the Army of the Potomac arrived on July 2, and circled back towards Washington, forcing General Meade to attack Lee on a place of Lee's choosing. This was the theme of *Gettysburg: A Novel of the Civil War*, by Newt Gingrich and William Forstchen. Finally, "what if" General Armistead's Virginians could have broken through the Union lines at 3 p.m. on July 3 and caused a panicked retreat by the defeated Union Army? The Union army may never have recovered the initiative.

In closing, I strongly recommend to all readers to plan a trip to Gettysburg. The battlefield is one of the best-preserved battlefields in the world. You can walk or drive and see the same ground as the soldiers did all those years ago. I suggest that you start every visit with a stop at the National Park Service's Visitor Center. View the presentations, grab a map, make a reservation for one of the excellent guided tours. Of course, no trip to Gettysburg Visitor's Center would be complete without a stop at the to the bookstore. Look for a book that will enhance your understanding of the battle based on your current level of knowledge, buy a children's book for your favorite young reader, and lastly, ask the staff if the sequel to "She's Just a Little Amish Girl" has been released yet!

About the Author

David is a retired custom homebuilder who has been a storyteller all his life. He is passionate about inspiring young people and teaching them history. She's Just a Little Amish Girl tells the story that he made up four decades ago to explain the Battle of Gettysburg to his young daughters and to inspire them to be brave and determined.

Note from David Bachman

Word-of-mouth is crucial for any author to succeed. If you enjoyed *She's Just a Little Amish Girl*, please leave a review online—anywhere you are able. Even if it's just a sentence or two. It would make all the difference and would be very much appreciated.

Thanks!
David Bachman

We hope you enjoyed reading this title from:

www.blackrosewriting.com

Subscribe to our mailing list – *The Rosevine* – and receive **FREE** books, daily deals, and stay current with news about upcoming releases and our hottest authors.
Scan the QR code below to sign up.

Already a subscriber? Please accept a sincere thank you for being a fan of Black Rose Writing authors.

View other Black Rose Writing titles at
www.blackrosewriting.com/books and use promo code
PRINT to receive a **20% discount** when purchasing.